SHENZHENERS

SHENZHENERS

stories

XUE YIWEI

Translated from the Chinese by Darryl Sterk

Cover design: Debbie Geltner
Cover image and interior illustrations: Cai Gao
Layout: WildElement.ca
Printed and bound in Canada.

Library and Archives Canada Cataloguing in Publication
Xue, Yiwei, 1964- [Chu zu che si ji. Selections. English]
    Shenzheners / Xue Yiwei.

Short stories.
Partial translation of: Chu zu che si ji, 2013.
Translation: Darryl Sterk.
Issued in print and electronic formats.
ISBN 978-1-988130-03-3 (paperback).--ISBN 978-1-988130-04-0 (epub).--
ISBN 978-1-988130-05-7 (mobi).--ISBN 978-1-988130-06-4 (pdf)

    1. Shenzhen Shi (China)--Fiction. I. Sterk, Darryl, translator
II. Title. III. Title: Chu zu che si ji. Selections. English.
PS8646.U4S4613 2016   C895.13'6   C2016-902309-5
                                                 C2016-902310-9

The translator wishes to acknowledge his wife, Joey Su.
The publisher is grateful for the support of the Canada Council for the Arts
and of SODEC for its publishing program.

Linda Leith Publishing Inc.
P.O. Box 322, Victoria Station,
Westmount Quebec H3Z 2V8 Canada
www.lindaleith.com

To the Irishman who inspires me.

CONTENTS

THE COUNTRY GIRL

It was on the train from Toronto to Montreal that she discovered China's youngest city. It was a charmingly sunny afternoon. She'd made it onto the train, breathless, a minute before it pulled out of the station. She needed to stand in the gangway for a bit to catch her breath. Then she walked into the forward carriage. She'd taken the train the weekend before, but this was the first time she'd seen it so full. She walked to the end and saw only a single empty seat, then hurried back, intent on claiming the seat with her shoulder bag before another passenger took it. That seat had been reserved for her by fate, she guessed. She sat down and unconsciously adjusted her blouse, slightly damp with sweat. Then she got out a packet of potato chips, a bottle of mineral water, and her copy of *The New York Trilogy* by Paul Auster. She ate the chips and read. At the same time, out of the corner of her eye, she checked out the occupant of the seat beside her. He was Asian, and he was resting his head on the window, as if daydreaming in the glorious sunshine. She'd made the trip by train from Montreal to Toronto every month for five years now, and this was the only time she'd ever walked through a carriage with only a single empty place, the only time she'd ever sat beside an Asian.

She lived in a village near Trois-Rivières, between Montreal and Quebec City. It was a ninety-minute drive from her house to Dorval Station, located on the outskirts of Montreal. It was to go see her mother, who was suffering from dementia, that she'd made the trip to Toronto. And she'd gotten on and off the train at that same station every time to avoid having to drive through the racket and the traffic of downtown Montreal. She thought of herself as a country girl and felt out of her element in the city.

Born in a little village in eastern Ontario, near the Quebec border, she'd grown up on a big farm. She was used to wide open spaces. She was used to the pace of life in the countryside. Even the country air, cow- and horse-dung laden, was to her a basic element of life. The university where she had studied was far from downtown. She'd double majored, in two language-related fields: French Literature and Translation Studies. To her, language was the most natural thing besides nature itself. She had loved language since childhood, and her passion had intensified her dependence on nature. "Every language is a capacious prospect," she once wrote in her diary.

Soon after graduation, she married her elementary-school classmate, the boy who always used to tease her. They had grown up together on the farm, and their families had lived together for a time. Right before their first child was born, her husband, who was an architect, had found a job with a firm in Trois-Rivières. They left Ontario in what was for her an exciting move, because she'd always hoped French would become a part of her daily life; another capacious prospect, as it were. At her insistence, they settled in a village thirty kilometres away from Trois-Rivières. In front of their farmhouse were miles and miles of fields, and out back a seemingly endless forest. She hoped their children would have an idyllic childhood like hers. The way she saw it, a country childhood was a happy childhood.

She'd been a housewife in her sparsely furnished farmhouse for twelve whole years. The aerobics class she took in Trois-Rivières every weekend was her only social activity. Over the years, her husband had often suggested moving to the centre of Trois-Rivières or even to a suburb. He thought the city, with its superior recreational and educational facilities, was a better place to raise a child. She felt just the opposite, and every time he proposed moving she was adamantly opposed. Eight years before, on Christmas Eve, her husband announced that he had quit his job. He said he couldn't take it anymore, he regretted ever coming to Quebec, he wanted to move back to Ontario, his only home. He'd rather live in any city in Ontario. Their daughter was not yet ten years old.

A chance opportunity allowed her to weather the marital storm, economically and emotionally, in just half a year. An aerobics classmate mentioned to her one day that the nuclear power station, which had just completed an extension, needed a French-English translator. The plant was less than fifteen kilometres from her farmhouse. No other potential workplace was closer, and French-English translation just happened to be her specialty. In the twelve years she'd spent as a housewife she'd sporadically taken similar translation jobs. She turned in her application and CV, got an interview, and got the job. The day she was given the contract she joked in her diary: "A marital crisis turns a housewife into a career woman."

Soon she had two serious admirers, which was no surprise; she had a fashion model's figure and movie star features. Maybe her legs and looks were due to hybrid vigour, for her mother was Austrian, born and bred in the Austrian Alps near the Swiss border, and her father was from the Scottish Highlands. Her fresh, youthful manner disguised her true age. Nobody would believe that she was the mother of two grown children and had spent twelve years as a housewife.

Between the two admirers, who were a contrast both in personality and in appearance, she chose the financial manager, who was half a head shorter than she was, because he also liked to read. She soon realized this wasn't enough of a reason, because their reading interests didn't overlap. He only liked Stephen King, while for her only Paul Auster counted as real reading. They had an on-again, off-again relationship for almost three years. The day they officially broke up, he gave her a copy of *The*

New York Trilogy, the one she would bring with her wherever she went. It was a relationship without passion, so they parted without pain. She didn't feel the need for it.

So she wasn't on the rebound when, two days later, she happily accepted when a brawny engineer asked her to go out on a date: a two-hour cross-country skiing outing in the woods behind the village. When the engineer took her home and asked whether he could kiss her, she neither agreed nor refused. And so they kissed a dusk-drenched kiss in front of the farmhouse, which delivered her into another relationship that was equally unrelated to her reading interests, and that failed to move her either aesthetically or physically. So, right before she went to Toronto that time to visit her mother, who was now mortally ill, she proposed ending it.

This time, breaking up had a subtle effect on her psychologically. She was tired of this kind of relationship—tired, it seemed, of relationships in general. She felt she'd need some time to recover from the funk she'd fallen into. Her mother's dementia deepened her depression. She'd only made it onto the train at the last minute because she had wanted to spend more time with a mother who didn't recognize her anymore. And now she was sitting beside an Asian man, the first time the Orient had come so close she could reach out and touch it.

Still less had she anticipated that this man would acknowledge her in the way he did. His eyes fluttered open, his head still resting on the glass. He was obviously taken aback, surprised that someone had taken the seat next to him. But then his expression changed, when he recognized the book she was holding. "You're reading Paul Auster!" he said in a weak voice, clearly pleased.

She turned her head to smile at him. This was the scene she'd been imagining and waiting for, for many years: for a stranger in a strange place to notice the book she was reading. But she never expected the stranger to be an Asian. "You know about Paul Auster?" she asked, trying to keep her voice steady.

The Asian man hesitated, then said, "Not only do I know about him, but I also like his work a lot." As he spoke, he leaned down and took a book out of his backpack, which he had placed under the seat, and handed it to her. "Look, this is the book you're reading," he said earnestly.

She found this incredible, because she didn't recognize any of the words on the cover. She opened the book and saw the same unrecognizable text. Then she opened it to the same page she was reading and placed the two books side by side. "Are you sure they are the same?" she asked. There was wonder in her eyes and voice.

"I often ask myself the same question," the man said. "Is a translation the same as the original work? Can a translation ever be faithful?"

His question seemed to challenge her. She was intrigued, but also disturbed. She also often challenged herself in translation, her chosen field of study, her profession. Could a translation faithfully represent an original? This was a constant dilemma. She didn't feel like responding to the man's query, even though she was sure the technical translation she did at the nuclear power station was faithful, perfectly accurate, and even though she agreed with Robert Frost about the untranslatability of poetry. She wasn't so sure when it came to other kinds of translation.

He wasn't waiting for her reply; it was a rhetorical question. "To think that Paul Auster would find a novel he himself wrote unreadable," he said, pointing at his copy of *The New York Trilogy*.

She smiled and returned the book to him. "Is it well translated?"

"I often ask myself that same question," he said. "Does a person who hasn't read the original have the right to judge a translation? It was through translation that I came to like Auster's novel, but was that the quality of Auster's novel or the excellence of the translation?"

"Auster wouldn't be able to answer these questions himself," she said. "Even though he himself was a translator, from French to English."

The Asian fellow said he knew. He also knew that Auster translated a modern history of China from French into English.

This was news to her. Again she felt both intrigued and disturbed. She felt as though the man sitting by her side was a true Auster aficionado, even though he had never read Auster's original work. "Are you Chinese?" she asked, curious.

He nodded.

Then she asked whereabouts in China he was from.

"Have you been to China?" he asked.

She said she'd never been to China. Or anywhere else. She said she lived in the Quebec countryside, that she was just a country girl who had never seen the world.

"A country girl who is fond of Paul Auster!" the Chinese fellow said, weakly.

She blushed at the conspicuous hint of flattery in this comment.

"What places in China do you know?" he asked.

She said all she knew was Beijing and Shanghai.

"Oh, yeah."

She then asked, a bit timidly, "Does Hong Kong count?"

He took a napkin and a ballpoint pen out of his jacket pocket. He drew a map of China on the napkin and marked Beijing, Shanghai, and Hong Kong on it. Then he pointed with the point of the pen at a place close to Hong Kong and said, "That's where I'm from. A very special city, the youngest city in China. A little fishing village twenty years ago, it's now got a population of more than ten million."

"I didn't know there actually was such a *young* city in the world," she said.

The Chinese fellow glanced over, obviously appreciative of her attention to his word choice. "Almost everyone in that city is an immigrant, just like here in Canada," he said.

She liked the way he said "just like here in Canada," giving her a perspective from which to imagine this youngest of cities. "So where were you born?" she asked, pointing at the napkin.

He tapped China's northeast with the ballpoint pen. "That's where I was born and where I grew up. In an old industrial city shrouded in smog." He paused. "I never knew the taste of fresh air until I left."

She blushed again. She felt as though he really cared about what she'd just said about being a country girl and all. He seemed to find it hard to believe.

They talked almost non-stop the whole trip, nearly five hours. She talked about her maternal and paternal grandparents, how they'd immigrated to Canada after the Second World War, and the different reasons why. And she talked about her parents. Her father had taken everything to extremes, while her mother did everything in moderation. They were quite incompatible, she said, but they loved each other their whole lives.

She talked of her two children, her lively, outgoing son and her quiet, introspective daughter. She said she didn't know how the same mother could give birth to two kids who were poles apart. She even talked about her ex-husband. She said that even after all these years she still didn't know the true reason for his sudden departure, that wanting to go home to Ontario and live in a city were excuses. She said she thought her ex might have homosexual inclinations. But she didn't mention the two admirers who pursued her later on, as if wanting to leave the impression she had focused her thoughts exclusively on her two underage kids after her husband left.

The Chinese man said almost nothing about his current life. She vaguely sensed that he felt deeply afraid of the present. He only said that he was a "failed artist," echoing the tone of voice that she had used for "country girl." He said he had begun painting at six, that his mentor was the most famous artist in his hometown. This artist wasn't only a mentor, but also a father figure. His study of painting was interrupted by the two jail sentences his mentor had to serve. The first time, his mentor was convicted of "hooliganism" for tracing Ingres's *The Bather*. The other conviction came when someone found that the painting that had brought him fame represented "the western wind prevailing over the eastern wind," which was the opposite of the Great Leader's ideal. He was labelled a "counterrevolutionary," like so many other victims of the Cultural Revolution. His mentor's first marriage ended the first time he got out of prison. Saying she couldn't possibly live with a hooligan, his wife took their two children and left. In fact, no girl in the city was willing to live with a hooligan. He ended up marrying a country girl a distant relative introduced him to.

"In China," he explained, "a country girl is a girl without culture, taste, or an urban *hukou*—a residency permit that allows you to live in the city. That country girl left my mentor while he was serving his second prison sentence. She couldn't live on her own in the city. She returned to her home village, deep in the mountains."

He spent a long time talking about his mentor, while she wanted to hear more about his own experience. He said only the most general things about himself. When he left the smoggy city, he went to college in Beijing, majoring in oil painting. After graduation he went home and worked for a time, then immigrated to China's youngest city, where he worked in a museum for thirteen years. And five years ago he made another move, this time to Montreal. "At first I didn't know what the city meant to me. Now I know that this is where I belong."

He made her feel sad when he talked of his sense of belonging in that weak voice of his. She also noticed how he turned his head to avoid the glare of the sun. She asked him why he had left China. He said he felt rootless, not just in the youngest city in China but also in Beijing and even in his home town. The feeling had intensified after his mentor died.

She found this explanation charming. "What's it like to feel rootless in your native land?" she asked. "Didn't you feel even more rootless when you got here?"

He gave her question some thought. "No, not more," he said. "It's just as much. I feel just as rootless here, a stranger in a strange land."

"So it's like the two countries you've lived in are a bit like these two books," she said. "They're the same book, just not the same." She was a bit proud of her analogy, and noted his reaction of pleased surprise. Obviously he thought it was an analogy worth being proud of. This wasn't the kind of analogy your typical country girl would make.

"Of course it's quieter here. I like the quiet," he said. "Not to mention the fresh air. In fact, the first fresh air I ever breathed in my life was here in Canada."

She looked at him, a bit flustered. "You should come visit us in the countryside," she said. "Then you'd know what true peace and quiet is like, not to mention really fresh air."

He seemed flustered, as well. He gave her hand a squeeze.

When the train neared Dorval, they both sensed that there was more to say. She said that, in all these years of travelling between Toronto and Montreal, this had seemed the quickest trip she had ever taken. And he said that he'd been in Canada five years and had never had such a deep conversation with anyone.

"All thanks to Paul Auster!" they said in unison." They each raised a copy of *The New York Trilogy* and touched spines. Then he tore the napkin in half: he left his email address on the half with the map of China, while she wrote hers on the other half. When the train came to a halt, he got up to embrace her, whispering, "Your hair is so pretty." His unexpected adieu soon convinced her that the encounter she had just had was fate, that the last empty seat in the carriage might as well have had her name written on it.

Twice the next week she dreamed about this fortuitous trip. In both dreams, she could only hear his weak voice; she couldn't see his face. This seemed odd . It was without a doubt the most romantic trip she'd ever taken. She hardly ever talked to anyone on the train, let alone had a heart to heart. And she'd never talked to a Chinese person before, much less talked about Paul Auster. This trip was a probabilistic impossibility. And coincidentally, she'd just ended the longest relationship she'd had since her marriage fell apart. If she had still been in a relationship, she wouldn't have been so curious about a stranger or let a stranger indulge his curiosity about her. These two dreams made her feel as though the trip she'd just taken hadn't ended yet.

On the way to and from work, and even on the job, she would suddenly hear his voice. She was expecting their conversation to continue by email. She was waiting for a note from him, had been waiting since the day they parted, assuming that when she got home she would find an email from him in her inbox. Custom dictated that he should be the one to send the first email. But when she'd waited almost a week without a word, she felt she shouldn't wait any longer. There had been nothing customary about the encounter, to put it mildly, so she decided to send the first email. The message she sent was extremely simple. She thanked him for the happy trip, and for the "friendship" that had already "budded." But just as she sent the message off, a message from him appeared in her inbox, saying more or less the same thing. She was excited by the serendipity and immediately wrote her reply. She said that the budding friendship between them would bloom and bear fruit.

They soon found a rhythm for their correspondence, two exchanges of emails a week. She had a linguistic advantage and wrote longer emails. And Paul Auster was the foundation of their friendship. She wouldn't forget to attach the latest miraculous line she'd read in a Paul Auster novel at the end of her message. In her fourth email she joked that they'd started a book club for two. And in his reply he pointed out that it was a book club in which only one author was ever read. She appreciated his understated humour. The greatest achievement of their book club was that she convinced him to try reading Auster in English. She knew she had succeeded the day he copied a sentence from *The Red Notebook* at the end of his email. He said it was the first "foreign" book he'd ever "chewed" through in the original.

The next step, the next challenge, was *The Invention of Solitude*, which she had recommended to him on the train. He remembered her telling him it was the best essay she'd ever read about solitude. He said that his two experiences of immigration, national and international, had given him the most intimate experience of solitude. Solitude was like a lover, had a double nature, at once angel and devil.

In her ninth email, she suggested that they meet again. His initial reply was positive and warm. He asked her when she was going to visit Montreal next and said they could arrange to meet on the platform at Dorval. Of course, it was a romantic suggestion, but she felt a platform meeting would be too rushed, and said she was willing to drive to meet him in downtown Montreal, where there were more possibilities. They could go sit in a funky local café. Or they could take a walk on Mount Royal. He was very happy at her "change of heart." In the following emails they kept making plans, as their next meeting got closer and closer.

She was surprised early in the morning on the day of their meeting to be woken up by the sound of someone turning off a car engine. She walked to the window and lifted a corner of the curtain. There was nothing in front of her farmhouse. It was another dream, a dream that didn't have a beginning or a middle, only an end. "It's just a devil, not an angel," she said to herself, in reference to the loneliness she suddenly felt. She sat in front of the computer and wrote him a simple email, saying the best place for their next meeting was actually in her quiet farmhouse. "You could come here for the weekend," she wrote. "You should really come explore my little world."

He didn't reply to her email, for the first time. She waited and waited, reading the last message she'd sent over and over. She regretted waking up at dawn. She regretted writing him that email before she was fully awake. What was "explore" supposed to mean? What about "my little world"? She regretted her ambiguous word choice and phrasing. Then she wrote him another two emails, just to extend him an apology, though not explicitly. In the first message she said that meeting on the platform at the station was actually a good idea, because they still needed time to get to know one another. In the second message she didn't even bother mentioning the "next meeting." She just said it'd been a while since she'd heard from him and was wondering if he'd started reading *The Invention of Solitude*.

Three more weeks passed before she finally received a reply. It was a single sentence, and it wasn't in reply to anything she'd written. He asked her to tell him her actual address. This sudden request took her aback, but also pleased her. Her first reaction was that his request wasn't because he wanted to send her anything, but because he wanted to appear at her farmhouse at dusk over the weekend. She didn't reply right away. She wouldn't want that kind of surprise. She would want to know when he would be arriving. She would need time to prepare her little world, so it would be a place where their friendship could flower.

She hesitated three days before replying. And then she wrote nothing in her message, except for her address.

Over the next two weekends she didn't dare to leave the farmhouse. But at the same time, she didn't want to stay home. She kept looking out the window until she suddenly felt a bit tired of the capacious prospect. The second weekend was about to end when she decided that her reaction to his surprising request had been wrong. Their budding friendship had not blossomed. He wouldn't appear. He didn't want to. There was no way he'd appear. That night, before going to bed, she archived their entire correspondence, clearing his name out of her inbox.

It was five months before she next heard news of him, by which time many things had happened. Her mother had finally passed away. Her job at the nuclear power station had ended early. Her son, who was studying international relations at McGill, had taken a year off to go to

Botswana to work. And her introspective daughter had chosen to go to university in Vancouver instead of closer to home. Her farmhouse was suddenly empty. And her daily life was suddenly empty, too. What was more, ever since she'd filed their messages away, her interest in Paul Auster had waned. She only heard from the Chinese man after all these other things had happened. And it was the very last time she would hear from him.

A notice arrived to pick up a parcel at the post office in Trois-Rivières. She didn't initially connect it with the Chinese fellow, who had been absent from her life for five eventful months. She assumed it was from her son in Botswana, a birthday present. Or from the executor of her mother's estate—her mother's personal effects, perhaps. But as soon as she saw the post office employee carrying her parcel out of the storeroom, she realized who it was from. From the shape, it had to be a painting. It had to be his painting.

The sender had not written his name or address, which made the provenance of the package all the more certain. She put the package on the seat beside her in the car. This way she could see it by looking over, as if he were sitting by her side once again. She couldn't really remember his face. All she could remember was his weak voice and their conversation. She couldn't figure out why he would send her a painting after five months of silence. She couldn't imagine what it might be a painting of, or in what style he painted. It was the sort of inexplicable detail of daily life that would provide material for a Paul Auster story.

If it were really a detail from a Paul Auster story, what would happen next? What kind of painting would such a sophisticated writer arrange for his protagonist to see?

It was a nude. A model was reclining on a sofa, looking straight at the viewer. Even with her limited knowledge of art history, she thought of Modigliani's *Reclining Nude*. A model in a seductive pose was nothing new. What was new was the identity of the model.

Yes, she herself was the model. She reached out, touched "her" face and seemed to feel the warmth of his memory. A failed artist had after five months remembered the shape and the subtly changing colours of her face, from forehead to neck. She was moved, and mystified, by his memory. What she found even more mystifying was how he knew about her body, which she had of course never revealed to him on that sunny afternoon. How did he know the shape of her breasts and the line of her hips? He had painted the part below the neck not from memory but from imagination, which moved her yet disturbed her. What were his feelings when he was imagining her body? The next thought was even harder to bear. Maybe the body in the painting was also done from memory: his memory of another woman's body, perhaps his wife's body. An excruciating pain seeped into her heart.

Anguished, she took off all her clothes. She seemed to see her own body for the first time. She compared the body in the painting to her own, and the burden of pain began to lighten, and kept getting lighter and lighter. She was sure the body in the painting was her own body, that this oil painting was the flower and the fruit of their budding friendship. She decided to hang it in her bedroom, on the wall by the bed. This way she could see him see her body every morning when she woke up. She held the painting to her breast, her nipples lightly pressed against it. She seemed to hear her breathing, and his breathing, too. Just then she noticed a letter stuck to the back of the frame.

She put the painting on the bed and drew the letter from the unsealed envelope. His last letter, and his first handwritten letter, to her. "Forgive my silence." She seemed to hear his weak voice again. "You must know how excited your invitation made me. But you might not know the pain I felt at the same time. Because it was an invitation I could not accept. Maybe you still remember, on the train, when you asked me what I'd gone to Toronto for, I didn't reply. I went to see a famous Chinese doctor. He was my last hope, but he told me that he could do nothing for me. This is why I was unwilling to talk about "now." My now is too fragile. Soon it will end. I am sure you remember I mentioned a sense of belonging. I meant what I said. Thank you for that remarkable trip. Thank you for giving me something to dream about, for the last time in my life. Since that day I have often dreamed of you. Even in sleepless nights, in which the pain is difficult to bear, I dream of you. The final painting of my life is a record of my dream. I call it *My Little Dream World*. If that's all right with you."

She hadn't cried in the longest time. Not like that. She

cried and cried as she re-read the letter. Their friendship had just budded, and she still didn't know who he was. He had not entered her little world. She wanted to know more about him, if he had a family, if he had children. She wanted to know why an original Auster would meet a translated Auster on the train. She wanted to know whether he had really entered her little world when he dreamed about it. Of course, she wanted even more to know about his now. If, at this moment, he was still alive, if he continued to dream about her little world somewhere out there in the big one.

That evening she sat in front of the computer reading all the email messages they had exchanged, and then sentimentally called up a map of China. She found the place he had lived in for ten years, China's youngest city. Reading about the city, she was surprised to discover there was a nuclear power station there, built with French assistance, that was advertising for a position in language training for technical personnel; they were looking for an English-French bilingual familiar with nuclear technology who could serve as a foreign-language teacher at the station. A job opening on the other side of the world was like that empty seat on the train. She felt a powerful pull. She pulled up her CV from the hard drive.

Getting off the plane in Hong Kong, she felt she had made the wrong choice. The humidity hit her right away—very unpleasant. What with the crowds and the towering buildings, she felt for the first time in her life like she was floating along, rootless. On the train into the People's Republic of China, faces pressed close, all Asian. But nobody wanted to talk to her. And she didn't want to talk to anyone. The flood of heads at the border checkpoint suddenly made her feel the fatigue and loneliness of the journey. She never expected she would be confronted with such a busy scene. She was just a country girl used to fresh air and capacious prospects. Waiting in line, she wondered if she would stick it out for the two years of the contract.

That was only the beginning, for once she was living in the city, she faced a flood of requests for her time. Nobody believed she was the mother of two grown-up children. Nobody believed she was a country girl who'd never seen the world. She rode her bike to work. On weekends she ran and worked out by the sea. She was a dedicated teacher. She was patient with her students. Of course her slim figure and deep blue eyes didn't hurt. All of which made the city curious, and curiosity led to requests. Almost every day she was asked out to dinner by people she knew, by complete strangers too, even if she'd told them she wasn't particularly interested in eating out. Lots of foreign-language teachers at primary and middle schools wanted her to "engage in dialogue" with their students after hours. As did the parents. An art school wanted her to model. A television station asked her to appear on a show. An exercise club wanted her to give demonstrations. Most persistent was a real estate developer who kept calling her, over and over, inviting her to his seaside mansion to "coach" him in English. She often didn't know how to deal with China's demanding courtesy.

One experience left her wary of divulging her nationality. As soon as people found out she was from Canada they would ask if she knew about Bai Qiuen and Dashan. She was tired of it. She'd heard about the Canadian surgeon Norman Bethune, known to the Chinese as Bai Qiuen, who had died in 1939 for Mao's cause and became a household name during the Cultural Revolution, but it was only after arriving in the city that she heard about the Canadian celebrity Mark Rowswell, who was known as Dashan, or "big mountain," for a role he had played in the 1980s in the most popular TV show in China. Who cared about Bai Qiuen or Dashan when the person who'd brought her to China was Paul Auster, an American writer very few people in the city knew about?

The demands the city made on her made her more and more homesick. She often dreamed of the simple little farmhouse on the other side of the world, dreamed of the row of Paul Auster's complete works on the shelf, dreamed of the capacious prospect from her kitchen window, dreamed of the snow and cold of winter, dreamed of the peace that went hand in hand with well-being. The nuclear power station was pleased with her work and wanted to keep her on for another two years. They even proposed doubling her salary. But she replied without hesitation that she just wanted to go home.

Before leaving, she accepted an invitation from a television station for an interview. The interviewer's first question was why she had chosen to come to the city to work. Her unexpected reply, that it had to do with an oil painting, made the interviewer extremely curious. His second question was what the painting was of, and the third came while she was still contemplating how to answer the second: "Was it an oil painting of the downtown cityscape?" "No," she replied. "It's a portrait." The interviewer was even more curious. He asked if it was of someone famous or just an ordinary person. She replied that it was an ordinary person. "How could a portrait of an ordinary person attract a country girl from Canada to come halfway around the world to China's youngest city?" he asked, looking right at the camera.

"Actually, it wasn't a portrait," she corrected herself softly.

The interviewer turned to look at her. "Then what was it?" he asked with the greatest seriousness.

She blinked, so bright were the mercury vapour lamps in the studio. "It was a little dream world," she said.

THE PEDDLER

I would think of him wearing his watermelon peel hat, a Chinese skullcap, even while solving linear equations. In a city where hardly anybody wears a hat, even in winter, his bewildering headwear always stood out. When school got out at noon, students would swarm around him. He would hunch over his two polyester bags to protect them, as they contained the two items on which his livelihood depended: popcorn and the sticky rice sticks the worst students called stun guns.

In Chinese class, however, my mind never wandered, though not because I enjoyed standing up and reciting the lesson, as our teacher made us do. I always hated that. It wasn't because I was ashamed of my accent in standard Chinese either; most of my classmates had worse pronunciation than mine, not to mention my teacher, a lady for whom even vowels were a challenge. She would read double vowels as single vowels, so that *ku zi de kou zi*—or buttons on the pants—

sounded like *ku zi de ku zi*—pants on the pants. This seemed like a reversal of the rhetorical strategy of synecdoche he had learned about—when a part stands in for the whole—because the whole (*ku zi*) now stood in for the part (*kou zi*). I found this reversal fascinating, even in my dreams.

We'd already gotten used to one other's accents. Why should I feel ashamed because I couldn't tell nasal and lateral sounds apart? I mean N and L. Of course, He-Nan is not He-Lan, which is how you say Holland in Mandarin Chinese. The former was a province known for its beggars, while the latter is European country, a major tulip producer in the world. I knew the difference between Henan and Holland! I never felt ashamed of my pronunciation; that never bothered me. No, the reason I was unwilling to stand up and recite the lesson aloud is that I didn't like it. This lesson, a well-known propaganda essay called "Who Are the Most Beloved People?" had galvanized two generations of Chinese people, but not me. My distaste for it started from the preview stage and persisted till the end of the term.

But I still haven't told you why my mind never wandered in Chinese class, not once. Because of Butterfly Girl. When she stood up to read, I would follow her rhythm, carefully attuned to the exaggerated intonation of a voice so captivating that it diluted the antipathy that the content aroused in me. Every syllable she spat, even the most explosive, struck me physically with its palpable warmth, pleasuring my auditory nerves.

Butterfly Girl was the best student in the class and the only one who couldn't speak Cantonese. I sat behind her. Two rows behind. Her fluttering utterances tempted me so much that my gaze would drift from the textbook, and I would find myself staring at her at her desk, sitting straight up. I didn't dare let my eyes linger on the realm between her neck and her behind, for my attention to that part of her gave me an intense and strange sense of shame. My gaze finally came to rest on her head, or, to be more precise, on her hair clip. Her hair clip looked like a pair of butterflies with overlapping wings. I felt jealous of those two butterflies. Why could I not be one of them? I started to imagine butterfly wings in her lovely hair. Out of a sudden excitement, I wrote a note, wanting to tuck it into her hand after class. The note said, "You are the *most beloved* person of all."

I worried the other students might laugh at her for her rapt recitation of the lesson. I didn't want her to be disgraced, wanted to save her from embarrassment. Its description of American soldiers was a far cry from the triumphant military heroes in the Hollywood war epics we had seen. In one of those Hollywood films, if you saw a martyr lying dead, clutching a grenade "spattered with enemy brains" in his hand, you knew he was an American soldier, and that the fellow beside him, whose brains had just gotten "blown out," would be German, Vietnamese, or Iraqi. And if a dead soldier had "half an ear" hanging out of his mouth, that half an ear definitely did not belong to an American.

Anyway, I used to get apprehensive that our class-mates would burst out laughing at her. But they did not. They stayed quiet. They seemed just as entranced by her recitation as I was. In my imagination, the overlapping butterflies in her hair were revelling in the mystery of life.

After class, the kids with the worst grades were argu-ing over who was the *most beloved* person in the Italian Se-rie A soccer league. The two stoutest fans in the group ended up getting into a fight and rolling around on the ground, as though dramatizing the combat scene from the famous lesson we'd been analyzing in class.

This eruption of violence excited the others. "Bite off half his ear! Bite off half his ear!" they chanted in Can-tonese, their pronunciation utterly different from the Mandarin, but interesting to listen to.

I did not know which side they were cheering for, whose ear they wanted to get bitten half off. In the les-son, it was half an American soldier's ear.

The two combatants found the cheer so amusing that they stopped hitting each other and got back on their feet.

One of them rubbed his ear, which was still in one piece. Soon, he and the other ruffians tumbled out of the school gate and crowded around the peddler.

The peddler had done battle with these bullies many times. His normally tense body seemed to tense up even more. He clamped his two polyester bags between his legs and crossed his arms, his right palm pressed against his in-ner shirt pocket to protect the money he'd made.

As before, the bullies instinctively divided into two pairs, one on each side of the peddler. The two soccer fanatics were now on the same team. They said they wanted to buy some popcorn, asking snarkily if there was a "minimum charge."

At first the peddler ignored them. But he got unnerved when they repeated their question. He warned them not to get in his way. He was doing business, he said, and he wasn't going to fall for the same trick again.

While the peddler was tied up with this first pair, the other pair managed to steal some stun guns.

The apoplectic peddler realized that he had been taken advantage of again. He stood straight up and nimbly grabbed the collar of one of the brats who had made away (but not far enough away) with the stun guns.

At which point the pair who had distracted him jumped at the chance to stuff their three plastic bags with popcorn before making a getaway.

The peddler noticed, but did not release his grip. He just looked over and shouted into the distance: "You don't know who you're dealing with. The American devils never slipped my grasp!"

The two bullies couldn't care less. They rounded the corner of the wall and found a place to stuff their faces with their ill-gotten gains.

Meanwhile, the other two students were trying without success to pry open the peddler's fingers. Struggling for dear life, the boy in the peddler's grasp tried kicking him a few times. He missed, but did manage to kick over a polyester bag of popcorn.

Seeing the popcorn spill all over the ground infuriated the poor peddler. He yanked the student whose collar he was holding towards himself, and another boy ran over and hit the peddler on the forehead with half a brick he'd picked up under a small tree.

Blood welled out of the wound and into one of the peddler's eyes. He let go of the collar of the boy he'd been holding on to, and pressed his hands to the wound on his forehead.

The remaining bullies made a run for it, kicking over the other polyester bag, the one with the stun guns, as they went.

The peddler strained to follow the retreating students with his other, unbloodied, eye. He was furious, but help-less.

Seeing his cheeks quivering with rage, I felt a chill in my heart. I felt sorry for him.

He turned round, leaned forward against the fence, undid his pants, and squirted a couple of drops of piss into his cupped left hand, with which he patted the wound on his forehead. Then he buttoned up his trousers, wiped his left hand dry on his pant leg, and looked in the direction in which the second group of students had run. "The American devils never escaped my grasp!" he shouted, then repeated it in a whisper.

His provincial dialect was very close to the one my mother spoke, which made the scene even harder for me to bear. I wanted to go over and help him collect the popcorn and sticky rice sticks. But I didn't dare. I was afraid the students who had provoked him would make fun of me the next day.

I saw the peddler collecting the sticky rice sticks, blowing away the dust on them, and putting them back in the bag. I saw him despondently looking at the spilled popcorn on the ground, as if he was contemplating picking it up, too. But he gave up in the end. He pulled the drawstrings on the two bags tight, tied the ends together, and hoisted the limp bags over his shoulder. Just as when he had come, except that now the bags were flat. He felt his forehead again. The blood had stopped. The wound was obviously still painful, but not as painful as the sight of the popcorn scattered around his feet. He looked at the ground in despair, and left, still hesitantly. Before he had gone a few steps, he turned back, and stomped a few times on the popcorn. Then he left for good, walking in a hurry towards the Huangbeiling area.

That was the same route I was going to take home. I followed behind him, wanting to know where he lived. I did not know whether he knew the lesson about the American devils we had just read in class. He had an obvious stoop. But he still walked very quickly, and it was not easy for me to keep up.

I had a sudden urge to know what his life was like when he was my age. Did he also have to do homework? Did he also have to take part in competitions? Now that he was all grown up, was he married? Did he have a son like me? I felt like I'd suddenly become more immature, because I had all these silly questions to ask. I even wondered whether his parents had ever imagined how he would end up, back when he was a little baby and they held him in their arms. And I wondered what exactly he meant when he yelled, "The American devils never escaped my grasp!"

If he had really taken part in that famous battle, he would probably know the lesson. Maybe he was one of the *most beloved people*—which later became a nickname for members of the Chinese People's Liberation Army. Maybe he himself had bitten "half an ear" off an American soldier. If so, then what did his illustrious past mean to him now? If not for the ignominy he had just suffered, would he ever mention his glorious past to anyone? I wondered how he lived with the memory. I wondered how he had become a peddler.

The distance between us got bigger and bigger until he suddenly stopped and started walking backwards. I did not know what had happened, at first. Maybe, I thought, I had been mistaken in imagining a glorious past for him. Maybe it was my imagination that somehow made him change directions.

But then I saw three young men in light grey uniforms chasing him. They caught up with him, and the four of them got into a vicious tussle. The peddler tried desperately to protect what he was carrying, but once again he failed. The shortest man stole both his bags. The other two pushed him into the fence along the road.

One of them jabbed his nose with a real stun gun.

I slowly walked over. I discovered that the peddler did not care about the two young men who were holding him against the fence. He was on tiptoe, straining to follow the short one's every motion.

Actually, he was staring at his two flat, polyester bags. "I need those bags to live!" I heard him shout.

"A guy like you doesn't deserve to live," the man with the stun gun said.

The one with the bags walked to a trash bin, slit both open with a knife, and pitilessly dumped the contents in, spitting three times before stuffing the two bags into the trash bin.

The peddler followed his every move with impotent rage, until he saw the man spit, when he looked away, shook his head, and slid down the fence onto the ground.

The short man ran over and tapped his colleagues on the shoulders, and the three of them walked away, laughing and joking.

The peddler sat on the ground for a while, as if dreaming. Finally he was jolted out of his nightmare to find it had come true. He looked around, dazed. He slowly stood up and looked at his hands, as if they had become useless appendages. He walked over to the trash bin, slowly pulled out one of the bags, checked the rip, and gently stuffed it back into the trash bin. He gazed in the direction in which the youths had left. His gaze terrified me and left me feeling empty inside.

The entire spring term was excruciatingly boring. Three of my classmates went abroad, one after another, all to England. Butterfly Girl went to Nottingham. One day a fellow classmate received a photograph of her in the mail. Her hair now fell loose over her shoulders. She must not be using the hair clip that had lulled me into incessant reverie any more. The butterflies, which seemed symbolic of the mystery of life, fluttered merrily through my mind.

The term was so boring that I would think of that peddler even while I was solving math equations, and I assumed he was must have died. Maybe he did not deserve to live, as the young men in the grey uniforms had said. I wondered whether he would look the same in death as other people. I felt again like I was regressing, becoming more immature, asking sillier and sillier questions: I even wondered whether he was still in pain from the wound on his forehead when he died.

When the autumn term started, the peddler returned. He was still wearing the same watermelon peel hat. He seemed not to feel the hot weather or the change in the seasons. Every day at noon when we got out, many students would crowd around him.

His reappearance was not a pleasant surprise for me. The first day I saw him I even felt angry, as if he had reappeared to refute my belief in his death. I was willing to remember him, but I didn't want to have to see him in the flesh on a daily basis. I cared less and less about the world around me. My love of math led to an obsession

34

with physics. I hoped I could live in a world where the speed of light was no longer an absolute limit, a world where time's arrow could stop and head back in the direction it had come from. I hoped that with the reversal of time my imagination could become even more free and unrestrained.

THE PHYSICS TEACHER

She remembered for a long time what her History of Western Aesthetics professor had said about the ideal woman. According to him, the ideal woman should have one reckless first romance, one hopelessly boring marriage, and one tempestuous affair, in most cases extramarital. Which was to say, an ideal woman had to experience at least three qualitatively different men.

She had chosen the course at random in fourth year so she would have enough credits to graduate. Like the other students, she knew the apparently pedantic professor was a well-known cultural figure. He wrote a newspaper column on current affairs. He had a flair for colourful analogies that made big issues seem small and relatable. International political disputes became marital spats and trade or cultural exchanges became encounters in an unsatisfying sex life. But she was totally uninterested in his talent. She took the course as an elective because she'd heard he wasn't strict on attendance and his tests weren't too hard.

He had not discussed the ideal woman in class. In class he ardently presented the most influential theories of aesthetics, noting how their authors were all men: Plato, Hegel, Santayana, Croce. It was in conversation during the break that he had mentioned the ideal woman.

She remembered him leaning on the wall in the hallway surrounded by happy young women. She remembered the strange emphasis he had put on the word "one." As though he himself had experienced not just one marriage, not just one love, not just one first love.

The students all knew he had a very beautiful wife. He let her have her way. Perhaps he was afraid of her. Which made sense, considering his claim in class to be a slave to beauty.

He said there was only one kind of slave who served justice and goodness, and that was the slave to beauty. He said that the greatest joy in life is to become beauty's slave. Maybe it isn't, or maybe he didn't, because two years after she graduated she heard that he had committed suicide. On Christmas Eve.

At the time she had found his definition of the ideal woman grating, and she'd already started to regret taking the course. She regretted it even more, now, disgusted by the class. She didn't want to become the professor's kind of ideal woman.

She remembered that a male classmate had voiced her own disagreement at the time. He had said, "If that's the ideal woman, she doesn't exist." He had also said the ideal man must not exist, because according to the definition, the ideal woman needed to experience three qualitatively different men. This classmate thought the professor's definition was sexist against men.

Maybe it was what the professor had said about the ideal woman that caused her to find love and marriage distasteful. She believed she would never be interested in men. The sacred profession she had chosen—she was a physics teacher—made her all the more sure of this. She often felt fortunate that she had made the most rational choice of her life at the age when her youth was about to end. She had become a science teacher at a little known middle school, but the classes she taught were legendary.

After eight years of teaching, however, she had started to feel weary. She quit teaching the extramural courses she'd taken on. It was as if only now had she discovered the monotony of her profession. She did not want to tire herself out. She had an impulse to flip through the yellowed pages of her History of Western Aesthetics textbook instead of preparing lesson plans for the following day. That old textbook contained traces of her youth, notes she had made at the time. Every time she flipped through it, she remembered her pedantic teacher's definition of the ideal woman. It still grated. She never expected that years later she would be relating it to somebody else, and in an even tone.

That person was one of her students. He had a powerful physique but a fragile spirit. His eyes flashed a stubborn frailty. He switched into her class the year she started to tire of teaching, and caught her attention immediately for his intuitive understanding of physics. It was a subject that had never come naturally to her. Even more special, though, was that he wasn't much interested in physics. He loved literature. He dreamed of becoming a celebrated poet whose name would go down in history. He said he did not know how he had come to have such a fantastic ambition. Maybe it was because of Yeats, he said. Yeats's poem "Sailing to Byzantium" had inspired in him a long-ing for immortality. He read world poetry like one pos-sessed. He knew all about the lives of the poets and could rattle off stories about them.

One day at dusk, he gave her a call. He said he wanted to discuss something with her, Faraday's law of induction.

She agreed that he could come over to her apartment in the evening.

He knocked on her door at the appointed time.

They both felt a little stiff and formal at first, but they relaxed as their conversation continued.

She complained about the family shuffling Mahjong tiles upstairs. He said that at his place they played Mah-jong upstairs, downstairs, left, and right, but that he didn't much care. He didn't notice noise.

She noticed that she didn't look upon him as a stu-dent, and soon realized that his reason for seeing her had nothing to do with Faraday's law of induction. He did not seem to have a reason.

She barely opened her mouth. She focused on what he was saying, and he spoke very fast.

Sometimes he was incoherent, his thinking full of vio-lent swerves and huge leaps. Most of the topics were unfamiliar to her. He talked about a poem that Auden wrote about Macao and about Gertrude Stein's apartment in Paris. He talked about Marina Ivanovna Tsvetaeva's exile and suicide.

She never thought that her mediocre apartment would be the setting for a chaotic discourse on such unfamiliar topics. It seemed to open a door in her heart, to arouse expectancy in her. Her curious gaze roamed over the emotional, voluble speaker before her. She was no longer treating him like a student. When her father called from Nanjing—an unwanted interruption—she frowned. Her father asked her what she was doing. She said she was having a conversation with a friend.

One week later, the student sent her a short letter. He thanked her for treating him as a friend; for "positioning" their relationship in that way, forbidding distance from existing between them; for making time stand still or cease to have meaning. He said he would curl up in the pauses in time and observe the spiritual light of language or silence. At the end of the letter, he attached a poem, which ended with the following lines:

> *On a river in the night*
> *Words throb starlight*
> *The oars of life*
> *Splash sadly meaningful sighs*
> *As if the flow of time*
> *Is an imminent catastrophe.*

This was the first letter she had received from him. She was not in the least surprised to receive it, because she had entered the same river in the night on the evening of his first visit. She had felt subtle emotions.

That evening, they'd passed through a poetic fantasy for about four hours. After he left, she calmly cleaned up the room. She seemed to see the trace of his lips on the teacup he had used. She felt embarrassment grip her heart. During his eloquent monologue on poets and poems she had become utterly absorbed in his lips, which in their opening and closing were not only deeply poetic, but also faintly erotic.

She put the teacup down. She did not know what to do. She felt tired. She had a shower and sat down on her bed, a bit lost. She did not want to read. She just felt like lying down. But when she reached out to turn off the light, she heard a tapping at the door.

Again she felt embarrassment take hold of her heart.

The tapping stopped.

She sighed. Her cosy room felt empty, for the first time. She turned off the light and lay down. Her mind was a mess, and she had lost the ability to think. All she could do was feel. Her body was like a starlit river on which a little rowboat gently rocked. She felt the leisurely movements of the oars, their melancholy striking of the surface of the stream. Like a cry in the night. She wiped away the beads of sweat on her breast that had suddenly formed, and quietly asked the endless night, "Am I old? Am I old? Am I old?"

Once again she started to look forward to class. But in class she was no longer just teaching physics. She started to care about the expressions and responses of the boy who had come to see her. She spent a long time preparing the lesson on Faraday's law. She hoped her explanation would satisfy his uncommon desire for knowledge and open a portal into his heart. She even hoped that he would notice and take satisfaction in her attire and body language. She felt bad about herself, as if she were a terrible actress trying too hard to please the audience.

One day, he spent the entire class gazing out the window. She felt guilty, not knowing whether she had made some sort of mistake.

After class, she wanted to go and ask him why. But she was afraid her concern might make him uncomfortable, might disturb the pure poetry of his mind. She knew how fragile his spirit was. She did not dare invite him to her apartment again. She was afraid that he would not be willing. Or that he would be willing.

The evening of his visit replayed in her mind, over and over again, which scared her. She was frightened of the throbbing starlight, of the sad, meaningful sigh. She was afraid of a recurrence. But she had to do something for him, because the next week he was the same. He just kept looking out the window, dazed, dim-eyed. She wanted to make him happy, as on the poetic evening in her room.

She still had not figured out how to make him happy when one night he came to her door again. He said he was just passing by and asked if he could come in.

43

She felt awkward because she had already changed into her nightgown. But she could not repress her excitement. She let him come in, and he sat in the same spot.

But this time he just sat there without saying anything.

She wanted to get him to speak, remembering how talkative he'd been the last time. She asked him if he'd been reading any interesting books, but he sat there unmoving, not saying a word.

She asked him whether he had written any new poems, but he remained rigid, silent.

She longed to ask him why he kept staring out the window in class. She longed to ask, but did not ask.

She suddenly thought of a Sunday in the bookstore when she saw a collection of short stories by Gertrude Stein. She told him she had found the stories hard to understand.

Still no response.

She didn't know what other topic of conversation might arouse his interest. She was discouraged.

Right then, she noticed her History of Western Aesthetics textbook on the shelf. She talked about her professor, describing his manner and his life and then mentioned what he had said about the ideal woman, leaning on the wall in the hallway that day during the class break.

The phrase seemed to have touched a nerve. The expression on his face was one of pain. He raised his head for the first time since he had sat down and looked at her with agonized eyes.

She felt uneasy. She felt as if his gaze might somehow

lift her nightgown. She crossed her arms over her breasts.

She saw tears in his eyes. He started to cry.

She wasn't sure how to react. She knew he had much richer feelings than she. She knew that his sensitive nature might magnify or diminish the significance of each and every word or phrase, leading him to feel desperate and isolated. But she did not know why he would start sobbing. She immediately explained that she had always found her aesthetics professor's definition of the ideal woman hard to swallow. She said she was not willing to be that kind of woman, that she found the very notion contemptible.

Her explanation made him cry all the more.

She didn't know what to do. She eased herself closer to his side. She felt he was a child again, a child with a wounded heart. She wanted to hold him gently, to let his head rest on her bosom, to calm him down. She hesitated, did not act. She was afraid her affection might hurt him even more. She reached out with her right hand, wanting to rest it on his shoulder.

She didn't expect he would push it away, stand up, and run out the door.

Again, she didn't know what to do. She felt an ache in the depths of her body. She covered her nose with her right hand and walked to the window, where she could just make out his distant form in the drizzle. Guilt tore painfully at her heart. She berated herself for reaching out to him. She blamed herself for mentioning her teacher's conception of the "ideal woman."

She lay down, sensing suddenly that she had now passed through two of the life stages described by her professor. Her reckless first romance had ended, and her tempestuous affair was stillborn. She was painfully aware that her dull marriage would never start, so that she could never become this woman. She still felt like her body was a river, trembling in the night. But the lost rowboat had turned into a dead leaf at the mercy of her trembling. A leaf without memory of time. It was so light, she could barely hear its undulating whisper on the water's surface.

The next day, a young woman was waiting in her office. She was extremely beautiful, overwhelmingly so. The woman said she wanted to talk to her. "I know all about you two," she said.

"What do you mean by 'you two'?" she asked, not understanding.

"You and my son," the woman said.

The physics teacher was shocked. She had not expected the boy to have such a young mother. The mother might even be younger than she was herself. Nor had she expected the mother would be so stunning. She wondered whether it was lucky or unlucky for a fragile spirit to have a mother of such crushing beauty.

"What happened between us?" she asked.

"He told me everything," the mother said. "You shouldn't have treated him like that."

"How did I treat him?" she asked, not grasping the mother's meaning.

The mother shot her a harsh glare and seemed about

to reply, but then changed her mind.

The teacher fixed her eyes just as intensely and stared right back.

"He's just a child," the mother said.

What had he told the mother? "I think maybe there's been some misunderstanding," the teacher said.

"You should have taught him the laws of physics, not talked about poetry."

"He's the one that talked to me about poetry. What he wants most is to become an immortal poet."

The mother seemed to turn into another person, though her look did not soften. Her aggressive bearing was now veiled by sorrow. "He's still just a child," she said, her voice quavering.

"His vain desire to become an immortal poet proves it," the teacher said.

"But because of you he has lost," the mother said in a trembling voice. She did not want to say more. What else could she say?

But then she added, "He came home very late last night. Soaking wet, from head to toe." The teacher felt the same ache from deep within her body she had felt before the mother arrived. But she did not want to let the mother see her discomfort.

"He still has a high fever," the mother said. "The doctor says"—she did not want to say anything more, but then she continued—"I asked him where he went. He wouldn't tell me. But it wasn't hard to guess," the woman said. "Two weeks ago he told me he was in love with

47

somebody. He also told me who that person was."

The teacher felt the urgent trembling of the dry leaf floating on the water, as if a wind had blown in from deep within the night. She turned her head and saw two dead trees and a grey sky.

"I don't want him to see you again," she heard the woman say. The voice seemed to come from far away, from outer space.

His reason for dropping out of school was that he was emigrating to New Zealand with his parents. Around Christmas, she received a letter from him in Auckland. He said that he had inadvertently mentioned her to the mother, and confessed how he felt about her. He had never expected the mother to get so angry, it was the angriest he'd ever seen her. She had said that love was the most sordid feeling, that she felt ashamed of him. She said if he kept on like that, she would rather die right before his eyes. He had been severely depressed. He never thought his perfect love would call forth such a violent reaction.

This explained why he had been staring out the window in class in the weeks after their first meeting. But it still didn't explain his own violent reaction, when she told him about her professor's view of the ideal woman.

On the second week into the new term, she got another letter from him, which he described as his "last word." He wanted to explain why he ran out the door crying that night. He said that, by her professor's definition, his mother was an ideal woman. He knew that many people thought little of her. One of his uncles had even said that she was the vilest woman in the world. But he himself loved her, a lot. He said that his love for his mother would be a lifelong spiritual support for him, that no one could take her place in his life. He also wrote that his mother was extremely complicated. Some of her experiences defied his understanding, though his incomprehension did not detract from his love for her.

He had given up poetry. "Next to an ideal woman," he explained, "all poetry is shallow." That's how he ended his letter. In the body of the message, he wrote that he wanted to return to the world of science, to rational thought. He would not write to her again. He hoped that in three years he would be able to transfer to the School of Medicine, en route to a career in surgery. He wanted to become a celebrated surgeon.

THE DRAMATIST

Every morning at 10:20, he walked to the eastern edge of the community garden to stand before the row of two-metre-tall pine trees. Rain or shine, never missing a day, he stood there for about fifteen minutes, his head slightly down, his hands hanging by his sides. He closed his eyes, but—judging from his slightly pained expression—he was not practicing Qi Gong. It was silent prayer.

The neighbours called him a weirdo. But I felt that *weird* was the wrong word for him. From the start, I felt that *eccentric* would be more apt. He did not seem to belong to our community, or even to this city, however demographically complex it is. He was the most eccentric person I'd ever seen.

Except for his dependable daily appearance at 10:20 every morning, he hardly ever emerged in public. And when he did surface, he had different effects on people. On the one hand, he always greeted his neighbours with a friendly nod, which seemed easygoing of him. But he never talked to any of them, nor would he allow them any opportunity to speak to him, which made him seem aloof. He'd been like this for almost three years. Nobody knew where he was from. Nobody knew why he was living here (and by himself). Nobody knew whether he would stay here.

His identity had unexpectedly been revealed only three weeks before. I had been resting in the hallway between classes, flipping through a newspaper someone had left on the tea table in the teacher's room. Inside, I found a full-page interview with him. I had never been much interested in drama, but it turned out I was familiar with the names of two of his masterpieces. The introduction to the newspaper interview said that both these plays had been translated into Japanese, Italian, and German, directed by famous directors, and performed by famous actors. It also said they had had rave reviews everywhere they were staged.

I don't remember how I got through the next class. All I could think about was getting home as soon as possible to tell my family and our neighbours about my accidental discovery.

Eventually, the bell rang to mark the end of class, and the city bus delivered me to the entrance of our community. I ran up to the first neighbour I saw, who was choosing mangoes from the fruit stand outside the little supermarket. I stopped in front of him, excited and out of breath.

Strangely, he did not seem the least bit surprised at

what I told him. I hadn't needed to say anything, I realized the whole community already knew the weirdo's identity.

The picture that went with the interview must be a recent photograph, because it was the way he looked now. The dramatist was shown in front of a bookcase, sitting proudly in a swivelling chair. There was a hardcover edition of *The Complete Works of William Shakespeare* behind him, the same as the one in our school library. Had he tilted his head slightly to the left, he would've blocked it. That was the only English book on the shelf, but it echoed the Shakespeare T-shirt he always wore—the only shirt he ever wore. There was a quotation, probably a line from one of Shakespeare's plays, inscribed on the shirt, just above Shakespeare's bald head: "No way but this."

Before going to sleep, I took a close look at the photograph and then reread the interview word by word for more information. The image of the dramatist, who stood at 10:20 every morning in front of the row of pine trees in silent prayer, kept appearing between the lines. Had the interviewer been one of our neighbours, he surely would have asked why he only came out at that specific time, and what he was praying for.

The first interview question was why the dramatist had announced his retirement three years before, when he was not yet fifty years old. Such an opening was no doubt intelligent and effective, because it would attract the interest of readers both familiar and unfamiliar with his work.

The dramatist's reply was simple and candid. He said that his passion for composition had already been exhausted by the drama in his personal life.

The reporter seemed to grasp his meaning, because he then asked the dramatist to explain.

It was obvious the man did not like this topic of conversation. He answered cursorily, saying that his life had been full of tragedies.

The reporter was not deflected and kept asking whether his personal tragedy was the true reason for his sudden retirement and retreat into a hermitic life.

The dramatist liked this question even less. He adopted a self-deprecating tone to point out that he had now begun accepting interviews, so how could anyone accuse him of being a hermit?

Thus ended the wrangling over private matters. But this brief tension in the interview raised many questions in my mind: What kind of tragedy was it? Why had the tragedy prompted the dramatist to retire? Why did he choose to live in isolation in this of all cities? And, why had he chosen to reveal his identity now, after living like a hermit for almost three years?

These questions made me want to approach the dramatist myself. He was not only the first celebrity I'd ever seen in person, but easily the most eccentric. I could not imagine how anyone could do the exact same thing at the same time and place every single day for three years. And I couldn't understand how anyone could greet his neighbours with a friendly nod, and yet refuse to talk to them or get close to them. I wanted to talk to him. I wanted to become friends with him.

I was sure, though, that he would spurn me if I were to take the initiative and walk up to him, I knew the best approach would be to let him take the initiative. Which is to say, I had to think of a way to attract his attention and make him curious about me. I thought of Shakespeare, or more specifically of *The Complete Works of William Shakespeare*. I really didn't like the inscrutable Englishman one bit. I still had not forgotten the Shakespeare course we were required to take in university, which I barely passed and would have failed without a make-up exam. But Shakespeare would be a bridge between me and the eccentric, of this there was no doubt. He would come to me.

The next day I borrowed the book from the school library. And the morning after, at 10:25, I took it with me and sat on the grass in the garden.

I deliberately sat less than twenty metres from the row of pine trees, and I took care to hold the book in my hands rather than laying it out on the grass. This way, I thought, the dramatist would notice the cover, which is to say he would notice me.

I did not expect to have to wait so long. I sat there for four days, and had basically read the whole of *The Merchant of Venice* before the scene I was waiting for was finally enacted.

The dramatist finished his morning's silent prayer. Walking past me, he suddenly stopped. "Are you reading Shakespeare in the original?" he asked.

I told him I taught English at the university, that English was my specialty.

The dramatist gave me a friendly look. "I can't read it at all," he said. "But I have the very same book."

I pretended to be surprised, as if I had never seen his picture in the newspaper.

"My copy is a present from a friend," the dramatist said. "As are the two Shakespeare T-shirts I alternate," he said, tugging at his shirt.

I was surprised that the book on his shelf was so intimately tied to his T-shirt.

"My friend sent me this T-shirt from Shakespeare's hometown," the dramatist added.

I could hear a sadness in his voice that he was trying to suppress.

"I never made it there myself," he said. "I missed that."

Again I heard the deep regret in the man's heart. I did not know exactly what he meant when he said "missed." But I nodded vigorously, as if I understood his longing to visit the bard's hometown. Then I mentioned the interview I had seen in the newspaper.

The dramatist humbly bowed and extended his hand to me.

I held his hand tightly, thrilled, not only because this was the first time I'd ever shaken a celebrity's hand, but also because I had fulfilled my wish to approach the most eccentric person I'd ever seen.

The dramatist patiently waited for me to relax my hand, and then solemnly asked, "Which of Shakespeare's works do you like the best?"

This unexpected question left me embarrassed. I was

too ashamed to say that I didn't like any of them. So I hummed and hawed and said I liked them all.

The dramatist could tell that this college English teacher had not done any research on Shakespeare. He let out an indulgent laugh.

I took the opportunity to take a step towards the man, and ask him which one he liked the best in return.

"*Othello*," he said without thinking. "Of course, *Othello*."

Of course? I wanted to ask but I did not dare.

He pointed to the words on his T-shirt. "My friend told me this is a line from *Othello*. It's what Othello says before he kills himself."

The dramatist's explanation unnerved me. Did he mean to say that this friend of his had selected the T-shirt, this gift, on account of that line? And why give someone two identical T-shirts? As if this friend wanted the dramatist to wear the present he was giving him every day, year in year out. Must've been a very special friend, I thought, ill at ease.

"I've done a bit of research myself," the dramatist said, "and 'No way but this' is translated into a Chinese phrase that means 'This is the only way out.' Is that the right translation?"

I said it was just a straightforward line. I couldn't think of a need to translate it any other way.

The dramatist frowned, as if disagreeing with my claim that the sentence was straightforward. "This the only way out, the only way out," he said over and over again. Then he turned and left.

That night before going to sleep, I was re-reading the interview in the newspaper once more, remembering our conversation, when I had a strange idea. I wondered whether the dramatist's preference for *Othello*—"Of course, *Othello*," he'd said—had something to do with his personal tragedy. I also noticed that in my previous readings of the interview I had missed a detail. The dramatist had mentioned a short story called "A Detail in Life" twice. He said it was a story about a young married couple on their way home from a trip. They came across someone supposedly familiar to the young wife, but of whom she had no recollection. By virtue of that inscrutable someone's insinuations, part of the woman's past—a part that was unknown to her husband—gradually emerged. The dramatist's comment on the story was that tragedy can result from the most mundane detail in life.

Just when I was revelling in my discovery, a neighbour called. She said everyone had seen me talking to the weirdo. They all wanted to know what I'd found out. For some reason my neighbours' vulgar curiosity filled me with disgust, as if they had invaded my personal space. I did not want to tell them anything. "He really is a weirdo," I said, trying not to say anything. "Weirder than you can imagine." I deliberately said "you" and not "we," as if I were no longer one of them.

Over the next two days, I was too busy preparing for my final examinations to go to the garden. But on my bus commute to and from work, I wasn't thinking about the weighting or difficulty of the exam questions, as in the past. I leaned my head on the window, thinking about our last conversation and imagining our next. I never expected that our next exchange would happen in a different time and place. For the next day, at dusk, when I got off the bus, the dramatist was standing beside the bus stop. "Are you waiting for me?" I asked, half in jest.

Still less did I imagine that he would pick up on the humour and reply with his own joke: "I'm waiting for Godot." (Though based on his serious expression and tone, I wondered whether he really was joking.)

The dramatist did not continue to wait. He walked with me into the community. He said that he had once written a one-act play about a city bus stop. There were no protagonists in the play, just people arriving and departing, as they did every day. He said that he wanted to express the absurdity of life by means of repeated departures and arrivals.

I appreciated the dramatist's mode of expression. I said that I often felt a sense of absurdity when I was waiting for and getting off the bus.

When we were approaching the door to my tower, the dramatist still seemed to have many things to say. He showed no sign of slowing down. Nor did I, as I also wanted to know what he had to say. We kept on walking towards the grass.

That's when the dramatist mentioned the interview in the newspaper. "How did you see it?" he asked.

I wasn't sure what his intention was in asking this, but

I knew I should not say I had seen it accidentally. I told him that I would never miss such an interesting story in the newspaper.

My reply seemed not to please him. "What I'm asking is: how many people have seen that article?"

I said that the newspaper had a wide distribution, and that practically everyone in the city would have seen it.

"You really think so?" the dramatist asked.

All the neighbours have seen it, I said, and all of my colleagues at work.

The dramatist looked up and gazed at the twilight sky. "Well, good," he said, though with doubt in his voice.

I did not know what he meant.

"Actually I just hope one person sees it," he continued.

I did not know what this meant, either. His rumbling voice made it seem as though he was talking to himself.

"After the interview was published, I started having bouts of loneliness," the dramatist said.

I recalled his "joke" at the bus stop. I assumed he must be waiting for the reader to respond. Waiting makes people lonely, I said.

The dramatist looked at me, lost. I did not know whether he thought I had it right or wrong. "I don't know whether I should keep on living here, in this city," he said.

I found this brusque. Our conversation had neared a crux of some sort, as if we had returned to the question he had avoided at the beginning of the interview. I did not want to miss this opportunity. I said he had to figure out why he had come to the city in the first place before he could decide whether or not to stay.

The dramatist looked at me, his eyes just as confused as before.

I still couldn't tell whether he thought I had it right or wrong. But I told myself that I must not hesitate. I mentioned the tragedy in his life. I asked him why he had avoided the question in the interview.

The dramatist seemed to want to say something. Then his eyes flashed. Something seemed to attract his attention. "Am I seeing things?" he asked, distraught.

I looked over. I did not know what he had seen in the twilight.

"Just there, on the path behind that row of pines," the dramatist said. "I don't think I am seeing things."

I also saw something, a woman in a black dress pacing up and down the path behind the pine trees.

The dramatist seemed to forget that we were having a conversation. He walked towards the trees, apparently in a kind of trance, but he was unable to get close to the woman. When he had almost reached the pines, a man in formal attire came to the woman's side. They exchanged a few words and then walked away, hand in hand.

The dramatist seemed shocked by this. After a while he plodded back, looking behind him. He looked exhausted. "I think maybe I was mistaken," he said quietly.

I had no idea where he was mistaken.

"I heard she left right after the telephone call," the dramatist said.

I did not know what telephone call he was talking about.

"I heard she came here, to this city," the dramatist said.

I did not know who had come to our city.

"Why would I have that idea?" the dramatist asked.

I had no idea what idea he had had.

"What does it matter if she knows?" the dramatist said.

I was totally lost.

"Waiting makes people lonely. Oh, 'tis true, 'tis true," the dramatist said. "Now I think I was wrong."

Wrong? About what?

The dramatist turned to go without taking his leave of me.

The next day after work I saw the neighbours standing at the entrance to the community, gossiping. When they saw me, they got extremely excited. They surrounded me. One said that one of the women had seen the weirdo at the airport while she was dropping her mother-in-law off. He had nodded to this woman in a very friendly way, but as usual said nothing. He was carrying a large backpack, as if setting off on a long journey. My neighbours asked me if I knew where he was going.

The woman's supposition was probably right. The dramatist had probably left, as the past few days he had not appeared at his regular time and place.

About a week later, I got an express parcel from Xishuangbanna, an ethnic minority area in southern Yunnan province. In it was a brand new tape recording with a label that read: "Why I came" in the dramatist's handwriting.

I could not wait to put the tape into the machine, and soon I heard the dramatist speak in a gravelly voice.

"My decision to retire and leave the city is indeed related to my personal tragedy. But there's a deeper reason for the tragedy itself, which only the people involved know. That's what plays in daily life are like. There's always a play within the play, and sometimes it's difficult to make out which is the cause and which the effect. I don't know how much responsibility I should take for the tragedy. But I know that it was a play I could not write, and that made me lose my passion for drama.

"In the past three years, I have revisited the tragedy from different perspectives. Through repeated comparison, I know that the telephone call is the best entry point into the story. I had waited for that call for four years, but when it came it took me completely by surprise. Thinking back now, I don't know whether the call came at the wrong time or just at the right time. My wedding was set to take place in two hours, I was busy with last-minute preparations, and a steady stream of calls were coming in, from my grandmother, my cousin, my aunt, the photographer, the manager of the cavalcade of cars.

"I never expected I would suddenly get that call. I hadn't heard her voice in four years. I was almost overcome. She said she had been trying to call for over an hour, and I could hear in her voice that she did not understand why the line might be busy.

"I hesitated. I still felt there was no need to tell her. I tried hard to steady my emotions, listening patiently to her. She said that she had just come back from England and had made a point of visiting Shakespeare's hometown. She said she had bought some gifts there and sent them from the local post office. She said that her purpose in calling me was to tell me to watch out for that parcel, and that she hoped I would see the stamp from Stratford-upon-Avon.

"That could not be her main purpose, though. This was the first call either of us had made in the four years since we (or should I say I?) broke off an incredibly passionate love affair that had lasted almost three years.

"What she told me battered my heart. I had not forgotten the meaning of Shakespeare's hometown for us. I would never forget. That was where we decided we'd spend our honeymoon. Now I was getting married to someone else. And she had just come back from that special place. I did not know how to react. What could I say? What was there to say?

"She did not need me to say anything, it seemed, because she still had things to say herself. She said that she had spent two days in that pretty little town, at an inn called The Black Swan. There, she remembered our life together, our "incredible passion." She said that at the end of her reminiscence she was still left with the same old question: Did I love her or not?

"After we'd first met she often asked me that. And she kept on asking the same question throughout our love affair. But after four years apart, this was no longer a question for me. She had to answer it herself.

"She told me that at dawn that day, at Shakespeare's grave, she realized that I didn't love her, that I never had. I reminded myself to hold my tongue. I told myself not to concern myself with her insult to my feelings. She had not finished saying what she wanted to say. And so I listened. She said she had thought several times of calling me, but had not been able to gather up the courage. She wanted to know why our incredible passion had come so abruptly to an end.

"She said that it was after that realization that she'd finally mustered the courage. Yes, that was her main reason for calling. All these years later, she wanted to know why I had suddenly left her, after we had chosen the place we'd spend our honeymoon. Whether I loved her or not couldn't serve as an explanation. She wanted to know the specific reason why.

"Hearing her state her clear objective, I was able to relax. I was certain she was just trying to sort things out, that she wasn't making this dramatic call out of nostalgia. That being the case, I thought she should be able to accept my present situation. I did not answer her directly, just told her that I was about to get married. I said that there was no reason for us to stay wrapped up in the past.

"She didn't speak for the longest time. I waited patiently and imagined her reaction. In fact, she was unable to keep her calm; finally, she spoke. She asked me what 'about to' meant. I said that it meant immediately. I heard

65

a grim laugh. She said surely I wasn't getting married today. My silence was response enough. She burst out laughing. She said this is ridiculous.

"But then her voice changed and became so very dark. She said that it had taken her four whole years to find the courage to ask me. She said it was just absurd, like the plays I wrote. 'Why?' she asked in her leaden tone of voice. Why had she, a little boat, run aground on such a ridiculous, treacherous reef? That's what she said.

"Maybe it's fate, I said. I thought that would console her, but it just made things worse. Furiously, she said she didn't believe in fate, especially not this kind. I did not dare to say anything more. And I did not want her to say anything more. Then she bellowed into the phone, 'You'll be cursed.'

"Her outcry filled me with dread. I asked her what she meant, as calmly as I could. 'Figure it out for yourself!' After she had finished shouting, she hung up. I did not think anything more of it. I didn't have the time. I had wedding preparations to finalize.

"Our wedding went very smoothly, and right afterwards my wife and I went to spend our honeymoon in her hometown. The package from Shakespeare's hometown arrived two days after we returned. I went alone to the post office to pick it up. I had decided on my honeymoon never to open it. I hid it on the top shelf of the bookshelf, behind my old manuscripts. Time flew by. A year of peaceful married life passed, and the fear aroused by that call gradually faded.

"One day, when I was looking at the calendar, I noticed that my wife had made a note on our wedding anniversary. I excitedly went to ask how we should celebrate our special day. My wife's icy tone and disgusted expression made me shudder. 'Our day?' she asked. 'That's your day, yours and hers.' I knew immediately something was very wrong. 'What do you mean by that?' I asked, on alert. 'Don't be so jumpy,' my wife said. 'You're more anxious than you were that day after you finished that phone call.' I did not know my wife had noticed the call that day. I was too nervous to speak. 'What is there to be so worried about?' My wife continued to goad me with her icy tone. I looked sideways to avoid her disgusted gaze. 'You really don't have to be so uptight,' she said. 'I actually don't know who it was. I just know you.' She did not complete her sentence, but I could guess what she was going to say. 'You said that a person can only have one true love,' my wife continued. 'That was just a line in a play I wrote,' I argued. My wife didn't give me any room for argument. 'Don't forget that you said all your characters are aspects of yourself,' she retorted. I didn't want to say anything more, and I hoped she wouldn't either. 'You don't love me, that's a fact. And it doesn't matter,' my wife continued. 'But there's one thing I just don't get. Why didn't you marry the woman you really love?' Her unexpected question reminded me of the call on my wedding day, and of my ex's supposed realization. What could be more absurd than that?

"'Silence is revolt against absurdity,' a character of

mine had said. I told myself not to say anything, but our conversation did not end with my silence; it ended with the package from Shakespeare's hometown. I'd always assumed that my wife did not know about the existence of the parcel, and didn't expect she would refer to it so caustically now. 'Didn't you say you wanted to celebrate our day?' she sneered, as if what she had meant to say was 'your day.' 'Why don't you celebrate by opening it? To see what's inside.' I told myself to keep calm. 'It's the perfect occasion,' she said. I told myself again to keep calm. 'You should open it.' Finally, she said, 'Whatever it is, maybe it'll give you inspiration for your next work.' Finished, she walked out.

"This conversation on the eve of our wedding anniversary set the baseline for the rest of our married life. This might be the curse which my ex spoke about on the phone. Our marriage continued for six more years. An unbearable six years. My wife just sank deeper and deeper into a darkness I was unable to dispel, and for the last two years, her nervous system was on the verge of collapse. She was unable to get a peaceful night's sleep. Sometimes she sat on the balcony the whole night and either zone out or whimper. My attempts at consoling her merely aggravated her anguished nerves. She had three serious episodes and had to be hospitalized.

"Many people had talked to me about it, including her parents, advising me to think about my own future. But I did not want to leave her this way. I hoped to help her make a complete recovery. Then maybe she would take the initiative and leave me. I did not expect that in the end she would choose such a violent means of leaving me. Maybe that wasn't a choice. Maybe it was the curse. At the time, I was away on a business trip. I rushed back when I heard and took a taxi from the airport right to the crematorium. Her body was waiting for me there. The forensic report listed her time of death as 10:20 in the morning on the previous day. When the personnel in the crematorium asked me if I wanted to walk a bit closer, I indicated that it was unnecessary. I had scarcely ever gotten so close to her body when she was alive, so what feeling would I have for it dead?

"That evening, I returned home exhausted. I fell asleep as soon as I went to bed. But in the middle of the night, I was woken up by a nightmare about the package. I had never opened it. While rummaging through my old manuscripts before I went away on the business trip, I had seen it there on the top shelf, seal untouched. But in my nightmare, it had already been opened. I sprang up and climbed on a chair to get to it. The moment I touched it, I knew that my nightmare had come true. I took it down. I didn't know what else my wife had seen. All I saw was a copy of Shakespeare's complete works and two identical T-shirts.

"What role had this package played in the tragedy? It's been three years, and I have still not found the answer to this question. In these three years, I have never missed a moment of silent prayer at 10:20 in the morning. That time of day is a curse to me. I wear that T-shirt every day. The deep symbolism is also a curse. Absurdly, my life belongs to these two women, to these hateful curses. One of the women decided I had never loved her, while the other believed, utterly falsely, that I had only ever loved the one who sent me the package. I couldn't write a more absurd play if I tried. So I retired—this was the only way out—and left the city where the tragedy of my marriage played out. The only way out. But why did I then move to the youngest city in China? That's the question. I was sure it was because I heard she, the woman who had said I would be cursed, had relocated there. But why would I go there because of her? What need of her did I still have? Yes, I did still need her, and only recently have I come to realize this. I also had to sort things out, just as she did when she gave me that call.

"There were two issues to be settled. First, I had to tell her why I suddenly left her. Only I could tell her. It was not just because of her call that I needed to do this, but also because a year later my wife, in a completely different tone, had asked me the exact same question. But there was another, more important need. I needed her to tell me what else was in that package besides the book and two T-shirts. Only she could tell me. Yes, after almost three years of hermitic life, I finally realized these two reasons for needing her. That's why I agreed to an interview, to reveal my identity. But then the waiting started, and I came to regret my public manifestation. I knew that she would not appear simply because I had revealed myself. We hadn't spoken in years, not since that call. She would never resurface. Which was to say that I could never know what else was in the package, what it was that had finally pushed my wife into the abyss. And it meant that she would never know (or perhaps she no longer cared to know) why I left her. Maybe this was the famous curse?"

There was a long pause on the tape. Just when I was about to hit stop, the dramatist's voice appeared again.

"There's no more need for me to keep living in the city. I will be staying in this little village far from the madding crowd for a week. This village marked the end of our last voyage together and of our incredible passion. We did know it when we arrived. The tragedy only began with the emergence of a particular detail on the day we departed. It's now been fourteen years since that day, seventeen years since the love affair began. It's been an incredible time. I've had an incredible life. I will move on my return. I will move to a place unrelated to either woman. The two women who have haunted me in life and death. The two women who decided I did not love them."

At this point, he choked up. He pressed the stop button, leaving a burst of static on the tape. If not for his overpowering distress, I believe that the dramatist would have gone on to tell me that one detail that everybody wanted to know. And maybe he had, and I would have learned it by listening till the end. But then I remembered the short story he had mentioned twice in the newspaper interview. I seemed to see him fourteen years ago. I felt as though he and I were the same person. I don't know whether he became my character or I became his.

Overcome with emotion, I pressed the record button and left the following lines on the tape: "That year, our passionate love affair took us to Xishuangbanna. Our trip would have been perfect, if not for that one detail. Our passion would have lasted, all the way to Shakespeare's hometown and beyond. But then, on the day of our departure, in the waiting room for the long-distance bus, a man who had just gotten off the bus glanced at us. He walked excitedly over, calling her name, which she found extremely strange. She did not know who he was. Then he mentioned another name, and she blushed. She seemed to remember who the man was. She did not introduce us. She asked him how the person he had just mentioned was. 'He … last year,' the man said. 'Brain cancer.'

"Soon, we got on the bus. She rested her head on my shoulder, while I just kept looking out the window. Neither of us spoke, but I could feel her sorrow. Her tears wet my shirt. Just as we were about to get off, she said, with a surge of emotion: 'You know how much I love you?' I reached out and touched her cheek. Of course I knew. So much so that, starting with our encounter with that man, I went on to suffer the most manic week of my life, drowning in a flood of jealousy, as his swollen corpse and I floated together into an endless nightmare. Tossed on the waves of our affair's incredible passion for three years, I had finally died. I knew that for me the only way out was to terminate our relationship. No way but this."

The instant I finished recording these lines, the telephone rang. It was the woman who had seen the dramatist at the airport. She asked me if I knew where he had gone.

I said I did not know.

She asked me if I knew when he was coming back.

I said I did not know.

She asked me if he would come back or not.

Again, I said I did not know.

THE TWO SISTERS

Hesitating between the two men who had been pursuing her for over half a year, the big sister chose the reliable one. Her choice surprised everyone, because the competition seemed so totally one-sided. The reliable one was so far behind his rival, whom the little sister had had her eyes on and hoped would become her brother-in-law. The rival already had a successful career and a glorious future. He also had dashing good looks and an urbane manner. He was the youngest executive in a communications equipment company that was planning an initial public offering.

Of course, his conspicuously superior qualities had not escaped the big sister's notice. It's just that they didn't impress her. They scared her. She could not stand how people would look enviously at her when she was standing with him. That kind of gaze sapped her confidence and gave her doubts. Besides, she'd always seen reliability as a man's most important asset. Career, looks, and deportment were mere decoration that she could do without.

The young executive was a catch, but he did not strike her as reliable. He had an overbearing self-confidence she found objectionable. He'd flaunted his sense of self-worth on their first date, when he took her to the café on the top floor of the city's poshest shopping mall. He talked nonstop, about everything from the Cultural Revolution to *Remembrance of Things Past* and *The Unbearable Lightness of Being*. He ended up talking about Vivaldi. He told her with certainty that he could do without everything in his life except for music, especially *The Four Seasons*, "that soul-gripping work."

His volubility scared her. As did his take-it-or-leave-it attitude towards life—music excepted. In her personal dictionary, volubility was an antonym for reliability. She had an instinctive distaste for talkative men.

After almost half a year of hesitation she finally made her decision. She chose reliability. Even though he was just a salesman in a real estate agency. Even though he wasn't cultivated. Even though he didn't look dashing. Even though he was twenty full centimetres shorter than his rival. Even though he fell short by far in wit and manner. Even though he did not like Vivaldi and had never heard of either *The Unbearable Lightness of Being* or *Remembrance of Things Past*. It was just because he struck her as reliable.

He never took her out for coffee or a Western-style meal, let alone a concert. He hadn't put as much energy into his pursuit of her as his rival had, and materially he fell short as well. But in his down-to-earth gaze she saw his sincerity, and she sensed a passion in him that made him his rival's equal. He didn't talk much, which made him seem relaxed and approachable. When he talked he seemed diffident. His slight stutter and tendency to blush struck her as transparency rather than a physical inadequacy. She especially appreciated how he never imposed his own will on her or quoted her little sister, he simply didn't have a will of his own. He agreed with her on everything.

Even on the topic of children, his answers signalled reliability. She had asked both of her admirers what kind of child they would like. The executive talked a mile a minute, as if delivering a painstakingly prepared report on bullish market indicators. He said he wanted a son. He wanted their child to grow up to be bigger and stronger than him. He wanted him to start learning the violin at age four to make up for his own lack of opportunity to take up an instrument. He said he wanted to attend his son's recitals and see him on stage playing Vivaldi's *Four Seasons*.

The same question had made the real estate agent blush. "I just want the child you would bear me," he stammered.

So she chose the reliable one.

Her decision had a lot to do with the pressure her little sister had put on her throughout the time she spent making up her mind. At first the little sister did not like the ordinary salesman from the real estate company, though it was more for his disposition than his position. She could more or less bear his diffidence, but she couldn't abide his lack of will. "Where's the fun in living with somebody who doesn't have any opinions of his own?" she asked with disdain. She was also disgusted with her big sister's criterion of reliability, which to her, was a synonym for mediocrity. She even claimed that "reliable man" is an oxymoron. All men are monkey spawn. Men prefer mobility, not getting tied down. She said the reason why men—actually, people in general—sacrifice their freedom and live with somebody else is simply to make life more interesting. "So there's no point in living with somebody who does not know his own mind."

So said the little sister, who did not realize that all of her hard work was having the opposite effect. The stronger her opposition, the more her big sister favoured the reliable one.

The older sister remembered all the mistakes that her sister had made in love, some of them several times. The big sister felt ashamed for her little sister, and she worried about her. Every time the little sister brought home a new boyfriend, she could foresee a fiasco. "None of the guys you have eyes for is reliable," she used to tell her little sister, with reprimand in her voice. "You're dreaming."

And her little sister had always hated the reproach. "Look who's talking," she said. "Who still believes she's found a reliable man?"

What the older sister found hardest to bear was that her sister did not see the mistakes she had made in love as mistakes. She said they were just part of her life experience, to be added to her "personal capital." The big sister blushed at her little sister's brazenness. She could not bear to let herself make the same kind of mistake, not even once. She believed that her life and her body should belong to only one man. One reliable man.

These two looked very different and had completely different personalities. This mystery of genetics had confused their parents and everyone who knew them. The strange thing was that their preferences contradicted their personalities.

The big sister was plump, and though she did not like talkative men, she herself was outgoing and sociable. She liked to meet new people. She would always take the initiative, warmly greeting the neighbours. It was easy for her to find a topic to engage a stranger in conversation.

Her little sister was skinny, and though she liked lively, talkative men, she was herself quiet, reticent, and socially inept. She walked quickly, head down, as if afraid that others would see her. She never nodded hello to the neighbours, much less had a deep conversation with any one of them.

The one thing the two sisters had in common was that they had very beautiful faces. But their different brands of beauty also gave people different impressions. The big sister's beauty was like a landscape that you could admire. People found it welcoming. The little sister's was like an oil painting, somehow distant.

It was because of the older sister's outgoing personality that the neighbours knew about their backgrounds. They were from Hangzhou. Two years before, when their father had died suddenly from heart disease, the two sisters left their temperamental mother and came to this strange city to live together. They soon found similar jobs to the ones they had in Hangzhou. The big sister, who had taken finance in university, was working as an accountant at an insurance company. And the little sister, a fine arts major, was working at an advertising agency as a designer.

Although the little sister was greatly disappointed that her big sister ended up choosing the reliable guy, she agreed to do the interior design for their new home. As it happened, she had help from her best friend, a graphic designer at a fashion magazine in Shanghai. The friend happened to be in town on a work assignment when the little sister was starting to think about the decor. Many of the details in the new home resulted from their frequent discussions. They used to be neighbours in Shanghai, and they had been classmates from kindergarten to university. They were intimate friends who had never kept secrets from each other. While discussing the details of the new home, the little sister made fun of her big sister's stubborn and foolish choice and her brother-in-law's feeble and in- sipid character. Her satirical commentary was so funny her best friend couldn't stop laughing.

The older sister had never liked this former neigh- bour. She thought this friend was a bad influence on her little sister's attitude and lifestyle, having made the same kinds of mistakes in romance and friendship. She was not at all pleased that her little sister was discussing the details of her new home with her.

The new abode was not far from the apartment the sisters had shared. The older sister had chosen the location mainly out of concern for her little sister. She was uncomfortable with her attitude and lifestyle. She did not like the friends—boyfriends and girlfriends—her little sister had made. She believed that if she stayed close to her she could keep her from harm, or at least reduce the risk of her making mistakes.

Her new husband of course had no opinion about where to live. After getting married he was as amenable as before, and in some ways his amenability to his wife's wishes stood out even more. For instance, he disliked going on business trips more and more, and would rack his brains to think of excuses to avoid them. This pleased the big sister no end. She knew that he cared about their married life and about her. She would not forget the time when he took her to a spring company outing that ended at a famous Sichuan restaurant. The company president had insisted on seating them beside him.

The affable president had had a lot to say that day. At one point he asked his subordinate how he had managed to get himself such a beautiful wife.

Her husband's face had flushed scarlet, just like the first time she asked him about his views on children. He looked down and did not respond.

"Attacking is difficult, occupying even harder," the company president had said suggestively, putting emphasis on his innuendo. "Next time I will teach you some key strategies, or should I say positions. You're sure to find them useful," he said, to hoots of laughter.

But her reliable husband did not laugh. She saw from

his fretted brows that he cared about her. It was because he cared so much that he'd never taken her to another company outing. She was thrilled, both because of his concern for her and because she had made the right choice.

Marriage had made the big sister even more beautiful. Even her little sister said so. And marriage had brought her husband amazing good luck. He was promoted to Department Manager, and the department he led soon became a pillar of the company. The president summoned him shortly after to inform him that his department would be merged with two other departments, and that he would be in charge after the merger. This was a transitional arrangement, the president explained. The next step would be an executive position; he would be a vice president.

His sales performance also won him the approbation of "the old leader," one of the three founders of the company who had later on moved to a seat on the provincial economic affairs committee. He had retired from his position many years before, but he still concerned himself with company matters and returned every year to offer guidance. On one of his visits, the older sister's husband made a deep impression on him. He deemed her husband the most capable department manager in the company. The first time he encountered her husband and heard him give a brief, he found the ear of the company president and said, "Talent like his deserves trust."

But the husband's success in his career did not affect how the big sister felt about him. To her, he remained his old reliable self, or even more reliable; with his success, they could enjoy a better standard of living. He did talk a bit more than before, but he was just as diffident, going along with her on everything.

When her pregnancy was confirmed, she proposed quitting her job. She wanted to be a housewife and stay-at-home mom.

Her reliable husband didn't disagree. He even asked her before the child was born if they should find a bigger home in the neighbourhood.

She was happy that their thoughts had tended in the same direction, and even happier that he had proposed the idea first. He seemed to have an opinion of his own for once.

Their daughter inherited all the big sister's good qualities. She felt relieved of a burden. She was so happy. When the little girl was a month old, she pushed her around in a stroller in the garden every day. She made at least five calls a day to report to her husband, who was often too tied up to get away, no matter what milestones their daughter had reached and whatever discomfort she might feel. When her husband did not have the time to listen, he returned her call when he was available. She saw the daughter as a heaven-sent reward for having made the right decision. She described her daughter as a little angel. She believed she was her most "reliable" reward.

Having such a bright little niece made the little sister forgive the older for her choice. She would make time to go over and see her every other day, and she gradually started to accept her big sister's insipid husband. She discovered he liked to talk a lot more than before. Sometimes he would enthuse about the new housing projects his company was developing. At other times, he was full of his daughter's latest triumphs. His consideration for her big sister led her to question her own criteria.

The older sister saw the younger's doubt and took the opportunity to urge her to find a reliable man and marry him—ASAP—rather than keep dreaming. "Look, think about how great it will be when you give birth to a pretty little treasure," her big sister said, her voice brimming with well-being.

The niece became the little sister's main topic of conversation in her long weekend phone calls with her best friend. Every time they talked about the little angel's growth and development. The little sister bought a fine sketchbook to record her niece's innocent postures and expressions.

Her best friend made fun of her, saying she was preparing to be a mother herself. "Have you met a reliable man yet?" she asked sarcastically.

The little sister responded the same way as she had to her big sister: With such a cute little niece, what was the point of having children of her own?

The little sister dressed the little angel according to her own aesthetic standards. She never hesitated to spend money on the girl, and planning her niece's birthdays was another of the little sister's prerogatives. The previous two birthdays had left her big sister and brother-in-law very satisfied.

When the little angel was turning three, the big sister asked the younger if she had anything special in mind.

The little sister said that she planned to rent a cottage at a seaside resort for her niece's birthday weekend.

The older sister thought this was a good idea. But she was not happy that the younger sister had invited her best friend.

"She'll be on her way back from business in Hong Kong. She'll be passing through that day," the little sister insisted. "She's always asking to see the little angel I boast so much about."

The little sister was not too happy to see how much her niece liked her friend from what she kept calling "Haishang"—literally the "seaside." She corrected her niece many times, explaining that her friend, or "auntie" was from Shanghai, not "Haishang."

But no matter what, her niece couldn't get it right.

Her friend didn't mind the mistake. "You said it right," she told the little girl. "I am from Haishang. Do you want me to take you to the seaside to play?"

The little angel radiated happiness. She was not the least interested in the birthday cake in front of her. She kept on asking how long it would be before they went to the seaside to play.

The sisters could not coax her to sit still and eat.

The big sister signalled to her husband to come and help, and he immediately put in a few words to try to persuade her.

Of course it was no use. In the end the "auntie" was the only one that could convince the little angel. She agreed to eat her birthday cake before going to the seaside to play.

Seeing her daughter had almost finished her piece of cake, the big sister felt irritated. And when she saw her husband, her little sister, and her little angel—who'd fallen in love with the best friend at first sight—all finish their pieces too, she felt even more annoyed. She herself had only had a nibble. When the little angel started clamouring to go to the seaside, she said she was tired.

The little sister could tell that her sibling was unhappy. The older sister did not express any support for her little angel, and although her sister's best friend was ready to set out, she just stood there, unmoving.

The big sister looked to her compliant husband.

His reaction was just the opposite of what she had expected. "Seeing that we've already promised the child, we should really," he murmured.

When they had just gotten to the beach, the little sister's best friend could not wait to take off her shoes and socks. She started to dance happily on the sand.

The little angel wanted to take off her shoes and socks too.

Her mother strictly forbade her. She had never let her daughter go barefoot, not even on the sand. To her it was uncivilized and unsanitary. "Today is your birthday," she said seriously. "You can't get yourself dirty."

Her husband patted her lightly on the back. She knew that wasn't a pat of support but rather an intervention.

She gave him a nervous glance.

"Today is the child's birthday," he murmured. "Let's make an exception just this once."

The little sister couldn't believe her eyes. She sensed there had been a sudden shift in the emotional balance between her sister and brother-in-law. One had tensed up, the other had relaxed. She also had a vague sense of what had led to this. She picked up her niece, not wanting the situation to get any worse.

Just up ahead, the little sister's best friend had already gotten a batik towel out of her backpack, which she spread out on the beach. Dusk had descended, but there was a lingering heat in the sand, in the sea breeze, and in the wash of the tide.

Everybody sat down on the towel. The little angel sat by her new auntie's side.

The little sister glanced at her older sibling and at her brother-in-law, realizing that she had something to do with the emotional reversal she had just witnessed. All she wanted to do was bring this special day to a close as soon as possible. She did not want things to get any worse.

Just then she heard her best friend point up and ask: "Can you see any stars in the sky?"

The little angel nodded and said she could.

The friend then asked, "Can you see any stars on the ground?"

The little angel was perplexed. She looked at her own

mother and father, finding them just as perplexed as her. In the end, the little angel's gaze returned to her auntie from Haishang.

"Don't you know that there are stars on the ground as well?" she asked.

The little angel shook her head.

"Well, there's you. You're our little birthday star."

The little angel looked proudly at her parents and her mother's little sister, and hollered, "Yay!"

Her father clapped for her.

Peeved, her mother looked away.

Mortified, her mother's little sister made a face.

After they had sat there for a while, the little sister's best friend stood up and walked towards the sea.

The little angel also stood up, wanting to go with her.

Her mother grabbed hold of her and told her severely that she was not allowed.

The little angel called her auntie from Haishang for help in a loud voice.

The little sister's best friend stopped walking and turned around.

Displeased, the big sister stared at her daughter and asked, "What are you calling her for?" putting a stress on "her." As if to say that whoever she was, she was no longer welcome.

The little angel started crying and making a fuss, trying to break away from her mother's grasp.

The little sister did not know what to do. She looked at her brother-in-law.

It was her turn to be surprised, when he impatiently said, "If she wants to go then just let her go."

Exasperated, the big sister stared at her husband. "What's that supposed to mean?" she asked in a loud voice.

The little angel took the opportunity to break out of her mother's grasp and run to her Haishang auntie's side.

"Don't let her go in the water!" the mother yelled helplessly to her sister's friend.

"If you're worried, why don't you go with her," her husband said in a low voice.

"I'm not going," the big sister said. "Think of how polluted the seawater is."

"Then do you need me to go with her?" her husband asked quietly.

"Why would you go?" the big sister said, disgusted. She felt like her reliable husband had suddenly turned into a stranger. She pushed her little sister to go over and intervene. "I really don't trust that friend of yours," she said.

The big sister felt unhappy at the sight of the best friend dancing in the tide, and she became even more unhappy when she saw her daughter not far away imitating her new "auntie."

She looked at her husband who was looking out to sea without a care in the world.

That displeased her even more.

Just then she heard her husband say under his breath, "It's her happiest birthday ever."

Worry flooded out of her deepest being, as never before in her married life. She worried her reliable husband had changed.

They sat in silence for a while. The big sister started yawning, one yawn after another.

Her husband noticed. "I'll go tell them to come back," he said.

But the big sister stood up preemptively in front of him, blocking the way. "I'll go myself," she said. She walked a few steps on the sand and stopped, yelling at her little sister to bring the little angel straight back.

Her husband soon stood up and walked to her side.

She glanced at him and noticed he was still staring towards the ocean. She also noticed that he had folded up the towel and was holding it in one hand. His other hand was holding the shoes that the sister's best friend had taken off. The big sister laughed bitterly. He hurriedly put the shoes and the batik towel on the ground.

The little sister soon came back, holding the little angel, her best friend following behind.

The mother took the little angel from her sister and felt the girl's pant legs with disgust, even though she knew the child had not gone in the water. "What man could stand such a crazy lady," she said unhappily.

Her daughter's little hands grabbed at her nose. "I'm not a crazy lady," the little angel said.

The toddler's reaction amused everyone.

On the evening of her return to Shanghai, the best friend

gave the little sister a call. She thanked her for her invitation and for making the arrangements. She said the little angel was just as cute as she had imagined.

But the little sister discovered she had lost any interest in discussing her niece with her best friend. She tried to listen to what her friend was saying, but all she could think of was her big sister's complaints. Her sister said it had been the worst birthday ever, and that the younger sister wouldn't be organizing any more birthday parties. The little sister did not relay the older sister's grievances. She admitted her arrangements had been less than ideal; but at the same time, she knew that her niece had had a very happy day. Her heart was conflicted.

Three weeks later her best friend called again. She asked her what she had been up to and why she had not called in such a long time.

The little sister responded coldly. She had lost interest in talking to her best friend.

The friend did not notice (or did not care) and continued on excitedly about the little angel. She seemed to know what the little girl had been up to in the past three weeks.

The little sister had a bad feeling. She did not ask her friend how she knew. She pretended it was nothing out of the ordinary, and even refrained from telling her big sister about it.

Then one day, three months later, she was in the café on the top floor of the posh shopping centre when she saw her best friend's profile, right before seeing her brother-in-law from behind. She immediately called her sister and asked if she had any time that evening to talk. She said it was important.

The big sister's reply was very difficult to bear. She said her reliable husband had gone to Kunming on business and would not be back for a couple of days. She said the little sister could come over.

The little sister went over straight from work. She told her not to bother with dinner, showing her the box of take-out she had bought downstairs.

After eating, the two sisters pushed the little angel through the garden in a stroller. They beat around the bush. The little sister did not mention what she had seen that afternoon. The big sister did not ask her what important matter she had come over to discuss. Back upstairs, the two sisters gave the little girl a bath and put her to bed. The little angel said some interesting things before going to sleep, but the little sister was not in the mood to note them down.

She helped her big sister clean up the room, and her big sister suddenly suggested she stay the night: they could sleep together in the master bedroom. The little sister was not opposed to the idea, so she followed her older sister's wishes and took a bath. Then she lay down on the bed, where, she realized, her brother-in-law usually slept. She found it absurd. After her big sister came to bed, she immediately turned off the lamp on the nightstand. She didn't say a thing.

The little sister looked out into the sudden darkness,

and felt a sting of guilt. "I'm so sorry," she said in a low voice.

The older sister took a long time to reply. Her answer surprised her. "What good does it do to say sorry now?" she said calmly.

The younger sister pushed herself up on her elbows and looked at her big sister, whose eyes were tightly shut. "Then you already know?" she asked.

"I regret that I did not heed your advice," she said. She reached out and patted her little sister's shoulder, indicating that she should lie down.

After the divorce, the big sister moved back into the apartment she used to rent with her little sister. Her husband, in the very last argument they had before separating, said that she could take everything except their little angel. She said she didn't want anything, not even the little girl in whom she had invested so much time and energy and affection. She had lost interest in everything.

In the three months after moving house she did not go out even once. Her little sister was worried sick. She advised her to go out and take a walk, even just to get some fresh air.

But the older sister was unmoved.

Then the little sister advised her to go and look for a job, maybe even a new boyfriend. "*Love* is vitality," the younger said.

Still the big sister would not listen.

Three months of confinement had devastated the older sister's body. She looked sickly. Strangely enough, her feeble appearance took nothing away from her beauty; it even lent her an alluring air.

One day at noon, when she was looking at her sallow face in the mirror, she suddenly thought of the weapons of mass destruction the Americans had failed to find in Iraq. A passion for retribution suddenly surged up from deep within her being. She felt resurrected. She told her younger sister that she felt impelled to take action. She said that hatred was vitality.

"Who do you want to get even with?" her little sister asked anxiously.

"I'm going to get even with whoever hurt me," she said.

"Any kind of retribution is only a retribution against oneself," the younger one replied. "It's the person who takes the retribution that ends up victimized."

The big sister could not understand what she meant. She knew that destroying a man meant sapping his pride and dignity. She said that she wanted the man who had betrayed her to lose all worth in the eyes of others.

"I never expected that you could be so vindictive," the little sister said.

"Isn't all of this your fault?" the older replied spitefully.

She finally went out on a Friday afternoon, and only returned the next day at noon. She easily conquered the company president who had wanted to teach her ex-husband effective strategies, or "positions." She had won the first battle.

The president understood her intention before she finished her first sentence on a public payphone. He told her to stay where she was, and he would be right over.

He took her to a Chinese restaurant in a five-star hotel. He encouraged her to eat to restore her health and listened carefully to her grievances, to which he replied with disdain. He said that his subordinate, whom he had held in such high regard, lacked even the most basic moral standards. He didn't deserve to be promoted to vice-president.

She pretended to be anxious. "Work and personal life are two different things. If he deserves a promotion, then you should promote him," she said.

He praised her for her magnanimity. He said that she was still young and shouldn't worry herself unnecessarily about her future. He said that in the future if she had any trouble, anything at all, she could come to him. He would give her any help she needed.

After dinner, the company president told her, a bit awkwardly, that he had actually arranged a hotel room for her. If she were willing, she could spend a relaxing night there, and he would come pick her up the next day at noon.

The big sister answered in an equally awkward tone, saying that if he would help her relax, then she was willing to stay the night in the hotel.

The company president grasped her hand and walked with her into the elevator. When the door closed, he cupped her breasts with his hands from behind. Excitedly, he told her he had dreamed of this day since the day he first saw her.

Her second target was her ex-husband's right-hand man, whom she had tried asking out many times before. Only now did the young man, who was eight years her junior, finally agree to have coffee with her. She had a strategy. She would not mention her ex-husband in the course of the conversation, as she did not want to pressure someone so innocent.

The young man forthrightly told her that he was hesitating between two girls who were pursuing him.

She gave him some guidance, like a big sister.

After hearing her candid advice, the young man said that he didn't like either of the girls.

She asked him what kind of girl he liked.

"I"—the young man paused with trepidation—"I would like to find someone like you," he said.

She laughed out loud. "Someone as old, or someone as foolish, as me? Or someone divorced like me?" she asked naughtily.

The young man bashfully looked down.

She reached out and took his hand, and asked him if he would go with her to see a Hollywood movie that had just started playing in theatres.

He did not say he was interested or that he was not.

She got out two tickets she had bought.

He followed her into the theatre.

About ten minutes into the movie, she put her hand

on his leg. She could feel how tense he was. She saw him stare at the screen, not moving a muscle. She thought he looked comical.

Halfway through the movie, she tried pulling at the zipper of his jeans.

He just stared at the screen without moving.

Then she tugged down the zipper ....

When they came out of the movie theatre, she asked the young man, who was still staring straight ahead, why he had always made excuses when she had tried to ask him out for a date.

He said he had been afraid.

She asked what he was afraid of.

The young man said he was afraid of losing his job.

"Some guys would give up the imperial throne for the sake of a woman," she said sarcastically. "And you're so attached to your job." Then she gave him a pinch on the behind.

Her third target was the old man, whom her ex-husband respected very much and always referred to as "the old leader."

She never expected that the old leader would already be so incensed on her behalf, even before she had parted her lips to complain. He started swearing about how her ex-husband was an abusive pig, an immoral little man. He said he had misplaced his trust in someone for the first time in his life. "And this was a major mistake," he acknowledged.

The old leader's condemnations and self-criticism

moved her so much that she started crying.

Her tears made outraged him further. He grasped her hands and told her not to be sad. He said that she should not concern herself with such a scoundrel.

The old man's care for her made her all the more anguished. She grasped his hand, and pressed it against her breast.

He trembled with excitement. Then he massaged her breast with a practiced hand, and with great emphasis encouraged her to keep her chin up and her chest out.

The old leader's reaction gave her another thrill of retribution. She placed his hand between her thighs, and he started dropping excited kisses on her cheek.

He kissed her and promised he would never let the pig get away with what he had done. Then when he delivered her to the door, the old man told her that, no matter what she needed, she could come and ask him.

She said she did not need anything.

He praised her for having not only a beautiful face but also a heart of gold. He said there were too few good women like her left in the world. He invited her to come to his house as a guest. He said that spending time with young people made him feel younger too.

Next she thought of the executive in the communications equipment company, her ex-husband's former rival, whose defeat in love had been an unprecedented boost for the reliable one's pride. She arranged to meet him in the café where they had met for the first time.

She arrived early to grab the table where they had sat on their first date.

She did not expect that all these years later, he would still have his dashing good looks. Still less did she expect the striking change in his personality. He did not look as self-confident as in the past. He no longer talked a mile a minute. He had become a good listener. Similarly, she had not expected that he would still remember every detail of their time together. While revisiting these details, his nostalgic expression filled her with remorse.

Her regret suddenly changed her attitude toward her chosen suitor, her ex-husband, the reliable one. She had ceased to hate him; her hatred had turned into disdain. He was just a bad decision she had made, not at all worth her hatred, she thought proudly. Her sudden change of heart healed her emotional wounds.

But she was surprised that the vanquished one was still so emotionally scarred. Well before she had finished her outpouring, his eyes were glistening with tears, which made her regret her decision all the more intensely in the depths of her soul. All worked up, she was anticipating his words of comfort and imagining how romantic it would be to lie next to him. She believed that if they were to make love, he would demand musical accompaniment, probably Vivaldi's *Four Seasons*. She didn't realize that what she was seeing was not romance, but abysmal despair.

"I'm sorry," the man said in anguish. "I can't help you now. With anything." He didn't provide any further explanation.

She did not want to know. It was enough that he was different from all the other men. She found his attitude deeply moving, which intensified her regret so much that it stifled her.

She rushed out of the café, out of the shopping centre. And when she had run several steps down the poshest street in the city, she suddenly stopped at a public payphone. She picked up the receiver and dialed the number at her ex-husband's new house.

This was the first time she had ever wanted to call him since the divorce. She nervously waited for him to answer. But all she got was a notice to leave a message. She hung up. She looked at the strange couples passing by, not sure if they were unmarried or husband and wife, or people having an affair. She felt suffocated.

She dialled the number again. After the beep, she calmly said into the receiver: "You know what? I don't hate you anymore. You're not worth my hate. Our marriage was a mistake. I never loved you. I only married you because you were reliable. That was my mistake. Now I just hate myself. Now all I have is a deep regret."

But the fact that she no longer hated her ex-husband did not end her reprisals. One day at a restaurant, she saw her ex-husband's biggest business rival. She remembered how he had described this man as a predator. She remembered the highs and lows her husband had felt every time they went head to head. She had only seen him once. But he recognized her immediately.

He took the initiative and walked over to her table.

A few casual words of conversation were enough to make them realize the opportunity. They quickly ascertained each other's needs. He asked her to come to his home the following afternoon. He said his home was very quiet, because his wife had taken the children to Europe on vacation.

She arrived as asked. And he took her right into the master bedroom.

In the next three hours, he brought her to orgasm four times, which she had never experienced in her married life. Those three hours were an eye-opening experience for her. They overturned her worldview. At the first orgasm, she realized her mistake. How stiff a man could get was the true measure of his reliability, she thought in the throes of pleasure. Riding his tremendous stiffness, she no longer saw herself as a victim. Thanks to her failed marriage, she now had an opportunity to experience true reliability.

And the man who gave her multiple orgasms credited his hardness to her. He said that she had given him a huge boost, gratified his pride. She made him believe that no matter how many times he had bested him in business, her ex-husband rival was a loser, a total loser. Three hours of passion did not tire him.

After the fourth orgasm, he let her lie in bed and rest. And he went to the kitchen and made her a hearty meal.

They kept criticizing her ex-husband over dinner. She was surprised that she could sit back and relax, beaming with pleasure. Her enemy's intelligence gave him an amazing dose of self-confidence.

When she said that her ex-husband was lousy in bed, he said, in a derisive tone of voice: "What kind of groundbreaking property development can come from a man who can't even help his own wife develop in bed?" He had obviously forgotten all about the psychological scars he bore from years of competition.

The older sister was not able to realize all of the revenge she had envisioned. After five months of insanity, her body hit bottom. She often felt dizzy and enervated. She would see blood in her urine. Her eyesight was deteriorating.

Her little sister noticed her decline and urged her to go to the hospital to get a complete physical examination.

But the big sister said she never had time, and was always making excuses.

Then one day, she arrived at the entrance to the community in a taxi, and after paying, she discovered that she was too weak to get out of the car. Only with the taxi driver's help did she finally manage to stand up and take a step. But on the second step, she fell to the ground.

The taxi driver took her to the emergency department at the People's Hospital. The doctor took a blood test and immediately summoned her family to the hospital.

The little sister hurried over.

By that time, the older sister was already in hospice care, and the person on duty told the younger sibling that the patient's days were numbered. They hoped that the little sister would be able to help them track the patient's sexual relationships in the past six months. They needed the names of all the people she had slept with.

The little sister immediately relayed her big sister's health condition to their estranged mother. She made a point of not mentioning what terminal disease her eldest was suffering from.

But her mother immediately guessed. She started swearing at the other end of the phone. First she said she had dug her own grave. Then she said it was punishment for her sins. She said that she did not want to hear any more news about her older daughter

The younger seemed prepared for her mother's reaction. She calmly put down the receiver. Then she called her best friend's husband.

His reaction was much less intense than her mother's; it was as though he seemed prepared for the news. He coldly said that the woman's life or death had nothing to do with him. He would not go to see her, and still less would he let his daughter go.

The little sister took care of her big sister alone for three months. And then she handled her sister's funeral arrangements alone.

The day that her big sister stopped breathing, her best friend called to ask if she needed any help.

She answered bluntly, "No, I don't."

It was on a day when she really needed help. She was so busy that she didn't get back home until one in the morning. She was thinking about having a quick shower and a good sleep, because the next day she still needed to deliver her sister's body to the crematorium. But standing outside the door to her complex, she suddenly found it all too hard to bear. The keys fell from her hand to the ground. She did not pick them up. She just collapsed on the stairs by the door.

The sound of her crying woke up the dramatist who lived upstairs. At first, he thought he was dreaming. He walked to the door and opened it a crack. The sound of someone crying downstairs did nothing to dispel the impression he was still asleep. Curious, he walked down the stairs until he came to the young woman's side. He asked her what had happened.

She did not reply.

He asked her why she did not go in.

She still wouldn't say a thing.

The dramatist hesitated, and then sat down next to her. He remembered a similar scene a year before. He had a powerful sense of déjà vu.

The dramatist sat there in a reverie until a cold draft snapped him out of it. He looked at the little sister. "Are you cold? It looks like it's starting to rain."

The little sister still did not reply.

"I've never seen you smile," the dramatist continued. "I hear that you have a charming smile."

"Says who?" the little sister asked.

"Says your sister."

"You talked to my sister?" the little sister asked.

"We talked once," the dramatist said. "It must've been about a year ago. How time flies."

The dramatist's words gave the little sister a funny feeling. "She wasn't living here at that time," she said.

"No, she wasn't. But she came here to see you," the dramatist said. "And it was at about this time of day."

"Why didn't I know about it?" the little sister asked.

"Because she did not want to bother you," the dramatist said. "She did not want to wake you up." He paused. "She was sitting here just like you, and just as sad."

"Well what did she say?"

"She talked about you. She said that your smile was charming, even legendary."

"I mean did she say why she had come to see me so late?"

"She didn't say it in so many words. But she kept on repeating these two lines. I imagine that she was wounded emotionally."

"What two lines?"

"She said that it's an absurd world, and that there aren't any truly reliable men to be found anywhere in it."

Hearing her big sister's famous last words, the little sister started sobbing out loud again. "She's already gone," she said.

"Where has she gone?" the dramatist asked.

"She's never coming back," the girl said.

The dramatist looked at the little sister, anxious. "What do you mean?" he asked.

"It's all my fault," she said.

The dramatist was going to ask her why, but a stifled rumble of thunder stopped him short.

The little sister shivered and wrapped her arms around her body. Then she glanced at the Shakespeare T-shirt that the man wore all year round. "I read the interview in the newspaper," she said. "When I was in the hospital taking care of her."

"You did?" the dramatist asked.

"At the time she was really out of it, drifting in and out of consciousness," the little sister said.

The dramatist let out a deep sigh. "If she knew who I was, she might've understood the answer I gave to her question that evening," he said.

"What question?" the little sister asked.

"What's the point?" the dramatist said. "From her tone of voice I could tell she was in deep despair."

"Yes, what is the point? I've been wanting to ask the same question," she replied. "What's it all for?"

"To me, it's for the drama," he said.

"Then what is life for me?" she asked anxiously. "And what about her? What was the point of her life? What was she living for?"

"According to Shakespeare, all the world's a stage," the dramatist said. "That's what I told her that evening."

"If it's a play, then it must be a tragedy," the little sister said.

A surprised expression appeared on the man's face. "You two sisters are so interesting," he said. "Funny how you both asked the same question and said the same thing in response to my reply."

"Isn't the play of life necessarily a tragedy?" the girl

asked, echoing her big sister's question.

"Shakespeare did not say that," the dramatist replied.

"Then who cast us in these tragic roles?" she asked.

"Us?" the dramatist asked doubtfully.

"Yes, us!" the little sister said, with certainty in her voice. "Including you."

THE PRODIGY

Only I knew the real reason why I did not attend the award ceremony. It was a special event organized by the municipal education commission for my teacher and me. I had come in second place in a national amateur piano competition, in the youth division. When the organizers of the award ceremony informed my parents, they said every media organization in the city would be there and that the deputy mayor, who was in charge of education and the arts, would give a speech and present me and my teacher each with prize money and a certificate.

But twenty minutes before the start of the ceremony, the organizers received a call from my parents. They told them I had a high fever and could not make it. They said I had gotten sick two days before. The doctor had done all he could, but my temperature just would not come down. They offered their apologies and said they could attend and accept the prize and certificate on my behalf. But they would not have the time or the inclination to be interviewed by the media. They hoped that the commission would understand.

The truth was that my parents had no idea where I had gone. At dawn they had discovered I was no longer in my room. They looked everywhere for almost eight hours without success. They had to make that call. They had to lie. They assumed I'd run away from home for the second time. The first time was when they refused to find me another piano teacher. That episode ended when they got a call from the Guangzhou Railway Police Office telling them to come get me. This time, though, they were wrong: I had not run away. I'd been hiding in the power room in the basement of our building since dawn. I decided to remain there until the ceremony had gotten under way.

By the time they were hurrying home from the ceremony, I was already sitting in my room. They were much relieved to find me there. They didn't ask me anything. They should've known that if they hadn't refused another of my requests, I would not have responded in such a way.

Two days earlier I had asked them to let me stay home from the ceremony. If they had just been more patient in letting me finish my explanation (which I'd even prepared beforehand), the situation would never have gotten that out of hand. But they simply refused, no buts. They said that even if I were so feverish that I couldn't walk, they would take me to the ceremony on a stretcher.

My parents approached the side of my bed together. They did not reprimand me or ask any questions. They just said it was a pity I had not gone. The deputy mayor had given a rousing speech. My teacher's account of my rapid progress in the past year or two fascinated all the parents and child pianists in the room. It was the climax of the evening.

I kept looking down, patiently waiting for my parents to finish saying everything they had to say. And when they were finally about to unroll the certificate and give it to me, I looked up and said what I would have told the whole audience if I had gone to the ceremony, "I will never touch the piano again. Not even if you beat me to death."

Thirteen years have passed, and it's as if it happened yesterday.

At the time I was only half as old as I am now. At the time I was a prodigy the whole city had taken note of. I was the apple of my parents' eye and the centre of public and media attention. I was a role model, an example other parents held up when assessing their own children, a pair of exceptional coordinates on the grid of achievement. Everyone knew that on the afternoon of my thirteenth birthday the mayor had called to congratulate me, that I had won a first-class at the provincial mathematics competition and another at the provincial composition competition. Everyone knew that I was reading Harry Potter in the original English. That nobody in town under twenty years of age could beat me at chess. That at twelve I'd not only memorized the surnames, given names, monikers, and places in the seating protocol for all the merry men of Liangshan in *The Water Margin*, but also read *War and Peace* and *All Quiet On the Western Front*.

At eleven, I'd memorized traditional Chinese essays like the "Ode to the Pavillion of Prince Teng" and the "Crimes of Qin." At ten, I'd discovered a mistake in the language test for the university entrance exam. At nine, I'd been able to extemporaneously report the surface area of Jerusalem and the population of the Republic of Sierra Leone, among other such trivia. And of course, everyone knew a lot more about my piano playing. Like at what age I'd started to play, when I'd gotten my first award, at what age I'd passed which examination.

All of these factoids had been reported over and over again in the newspapers. So parents who wanted to force their children to study the piano used my progress to measure their own children and make demands on them. I was a famous local wunderkind, and the most amazing thing about me was that I didn't appear to have any of the weird afflictions that tend to plague other prodigies: paranoia, depression or isolation, eccentricity. Everyone thought I was a healthy kid, mentally and physically. I took part in student government. I was a volunteer at the bookstore and the library. I was very polite to my neighbours. And I was modest in front of my classmates. In a word, I was a well-rounded wunderkind, a healthy, happy prodigy. Or so everyone thought.

Only I knew how ignorant all of these people were about me, including my parents. They did not see, nor could they see, the darkness behind the brilliant façade of my life. And they could not know that for a half a year around my thirteenth birthday I'd had a series of very strange experiences, in which I'd met first an angel and then a devil, and suffered mental and physical tumult and torment.

Nobody knew about this. And nobody would have wanted to know. The award ceremony was an opportunity to let everyone know how little they all knew about me. But I suddenly withdrew. I begged my parents to let me stay home. I was all of a sudden unwilling to reveal my trauma to others.

But my parents did not have the patience to let me finish my explanation. They said it was an award ceremony held for me. I had to go. They would be humiliated if I did not go.

They did not know that true humiliation would await them if I went.

Had I gone to the award ceremony, I would have told everyone how I'd met an angel fifteen years older than me. She was my cousin. She arrived in a hurry one evening from Shilong, about a three-hour train ride north of our city. There was no light in her face and no life in her eyes. She looked worn out.

I had not seen my cousin in two years. I had not thought that she could change so drastically in such a short time. She was no longer just my cousin, an innocent girl. She had become a woman, a source of temptation. Even though she looked exhausted, I could still smell a particular aroma on her. It was a kind of message she was sending from deep in her womanly being.

The gentle touch of her hand on my head sent a thrilling and embarrassing palpitation through my body.

At night my mother told me to turn off the light and go to sleep. She also said that my cousin was going to stay with us for a while.

When I asked her why, she said that she couldn't go on living in her own house anymore.

I again asked why, and my mother asked if I had noticed the scar on my cousin's left cheek.

It was conspicuous. Of course I had seen it.

Mother said my cousin's husband had made that mark by hitting her with a boiling hot spatula.

I asked why her husband would do such a thing.

My mother said she did not know and did not want to know. She reminded me never to ask my cousin about the scar.

My cousin stayed with us for two weeks, during which time my mother arranged for me to sleep on the couch in the living room while my cousin slept in my bed.

Every night for those two weeks I had difficulty getting to sleep. As I tossed and turned, I would hear my cousin tossing and turning in my bed, too. This correspondence made me feel that the night wasn't just a time, but also a space where we could be together, both then and in the future.

Many times I envisioned a future in which we could be alone together. I saw myself as a dashing youth, while my cousin was still just as young and pretty as she was when I was thirteen. She would be wearing a brightly coloured apron as she brought out my favourite dishes: spicy hot tofu and steamed breaded pork chops. I would stare at her pale white arms, as another of those thrilling and embarrassing palpitations coursed through my body.

It was the most amazing two weeks of my life. My nocturnal excitement and agitation left me dazed during the day. I could not focus on anything. No matter whether it was on the blackboard, on the sheet music, or in the sky. Everywhere I looked I saw an image of my cousin. A bead of sweat on the tip of her nose. The curves at the corner of her mouth. Her billowing hair, her swelling breasts. The tempting crevice between her upper and lower arms when she pressed them together. Every day after school I would rush home as fast as I could, to be with her as quickly as possible. I wanted to smell that womanly scent emanating out of her deepest being.

One Friday evening, my parents went to the hospital to see a colleague who had had a sudden stroke. They ate dinner in a rush and left.

This was the first time (and as it turned out, the only time) I had ever been alone with my cousin. I deliberately ate slowly, because I didn't want my miraculous meal with her to end. Every time our eyes met, a tender smile would appear on her face. I felt as though that smile belonged to me and me alone. To me that smile was the acme of beauty, a kind that even music could not convey, and that no one else could appreciate. I was infatuated. I felt I'd stepped into the world of tomorrow to become a handsome young man.

115

"Why did he hit you?" I asked brusquely, incensed.

My cousin smiled at me, but did not seem to think this was a question I should be asking. "Because"—she paused—"because he knows I don't love him."

I never imagined that my cousin would respond in this way. "If you didn't love him why did you get married?" I asked.

My cousin put down her chopsticks, and leaned back in her chair. "I don't know," she said. "Not everything in life has a why."

But that didn't stop me. I had many other questions to ask, many more whys. "Then why don't you get a divorce?" I asked.

My cousin looked me in the eye. "Because he doesn't want to get a divorce," she said helplessly.

I was even sadder than she. I could not understand how anyone could stand being trapped in a relationship like that. "Have you never loved him?" I asked.

My cousin looked distressed. She nodded and said, "I love someone else."

This mention of someone else was a comfort to me. It was as if that someone else was myself. "Then why didn't you get married to this someone else?" I couldn't wait to ask.

"Because I could not get married to him," she said.

"Why not?"

"Because he died," my cousin said, distraught. "Because he's already dead."

Her revelation chilled me to the bone. I did not dare

ask any other questions. I did not want to make my cousin unhappy. I looked down, thinking of the first corpse I had seen, a junior high school student who had drowned in the reservoir. I was only seven years old at the time. I had squeezed through the onlookers and seen an alabaster body, and I realized then how terrifying death was, even when it was a complete stranger. How terrifying the death of a loved one would be!

Nobody knew about our conversation. Still less did anyone know about the emotional and psychological effect it would have on me and my life. Love and death had met in my heart, engendering a depression and terror that I've never been able to escape.

That evening, under the influence of the emotional shock, I practiced Bach's *Goldberg Variations*. As I was practicing the sixteenth variation, I heard a mysterious voice from deep within the music. "He's not dead, he's not dead, he's not dead," the voice kept repeating for a full minute. It conveyed to me the sublimity of the music and the majesty of my performance. I vowed to practice all the harder to win a prize in the next piano competition, just as everyone expected me to do. I wanted to comfort the wounded angel with an honour, to send a secret message to my cousin—that the man she loved was not dead, that he was growing into a man at an amazing pace.

The sound of the toilet flushing interrupted my thoughts. I noticed that my cousin had just gone to the bathroom. To notice such a thing seemed so vulgar of me that I stopped playing, plunged into shame. I stuck my cheek on the piano keys. I had to escape that shame.

But then, the sound of water appeared again; my cousin was about to take a shower. I became conscious of her taking off all her clothes. I heard the sound of the shower curtain and of the water ricocheting off her body onto the curtain. Shame immediately yielded to a powerful curiosity.

I slowly left the piano bench, walked out of the room, and gently pressed my face against the frosted glass door of the bathroom. I couldn't see a thing; but I could hear. I could hear in the fluctuations in the sound of the water the changes in my cousin's posture. Those shifts, full of temptation, made me palpitate violently from head to toe. I was on the verge of collapse. I felt a powerful cramping in the lower left half of my abdomen. A spasm of heat spurt out of my body. I felt ashamed.

I only saw my cousin's husband once. The time he came to take her away. He looked just as my relatives described him, cultivated and educated. I could not associate him with the person who had smacked her across the face with a boiling hot spatula. As I watched him take my cousin away—or I should say, as I watched my cousin leave with him—I felt an intense hatred. Not for the person who took away my angel, mind you; the person I hated was my angel. "Why is she going with him?" I asked my mother in despair.

My mother said, distractedly, "She's going home."

This vague answer cut my wounded heart like a knife. "That's not her home," I said.

"What do you mean by that?" my mother asked, still distracted. "Then tell me, where is her home?"

I looked down. I knew I could not tell her that my cousin's home was far away, in the future. I could not say that her home was my home. I hated my cousin! I could not forgive her for suddenly abandoning me, for leaving with someone she did not love. I could not forgive her for turning my first love into my first loss in love.

This was thirteen years ago, but I remember it all clear as day.

Had I gone to the ceremony, I would have pointed at the bald guy standing beside me, and cried out: "It's him!" He was my teacher and mentor, a fact that everybody knew. Yet had I appeared at the award ceremony, I would have let everybody know that he was also the devil who had almost dragged me down into hell.

What brought us together was the provincial youth piano competition. He was one of the judges, and I was the youngest prizewinner, not yet eleven years old at the time. After the competition ended, he walked over to my parents, full of praise, and said that he wanted to take me on as his pupil. My parents were thrilled, because he was a teacher with a good reputation, and all parents dreamed of their children receiving instruction from him. His eagerness to take me on was not just an assessment of my present talents, but also a prophecy of my future triumphs.

Indeed, after a year of instruction, I had made rapid

progress. It was a happy year, an ordinary year. During every class, my mother would sit beside me, and afterwards give a detailed summary of the famous teacher's lesson, assessing his pedagogy. She said that I was so lucky to be able to receive such expert instruction. And she had just as much praise for my progress as well. My mother even reassessed her initial reserve about my prospects as a pianist. She felt ever more certain that piano should be my lifelong profession.

But then the next summer, things went awry. My mother told me one day that so self-aware an adolescent as me should not need his mother to sit in on every lesson. Later on I learned that this was the devil's own recommendation. My mother did as my teacher said. She described it as "training" for me—an abnormal training regime, as it turned out.

I soon noticed that the devil treated me very differently when my mother was not there. In her absence, he became much more affectionate, even passionate. There was a lot of hand touching. He would often put his arm around my shoulders and start stroking my back. And when the lesson was over, rather than a simple pat on the head, he would hold me tightly for the longest time, before finally saying goodbye.

The impact my cousin had on me did not escape the devil's notice. During those amazing two weeks when my cousin stayed with us, he had a temper tantrum every lesson. He reprimanded me for my lack of focus, for seeming to allow my eyes to drift from the music. Yet in the week after my cousin broke my heart, when I was in an even poorer state, the devil seemed extremely accommodating, as if he knew that a change had occurred in my life. He appeared quite pleased that I had experienced such a loss of love. It was like schadenfreude.

One day, for the first time, he put his hand on my thigh, and began to demonstrate the fingering and forcefulness with his fat fingers.

The feel of his fingers on my skin left me queasy. But I did not dare resist him, as he said that this was a particularly effective method he had invented.

He said that a demonstration on my leg would make it easier for me to remember the various techniques, because of the nervous connection between my thigh and my brain. After practice that day, the eager devil not only held me tightly, but gave me a kiss on the lips.

I felt powerfully ashamed.

That day, I rushed home, wanting to tell my mother immediately about the weird things that the devil had done. But the instant I got home, I felt so overcome with shame that I changed my mind. I feared my mother would criticize me or laugh at me. I was even more afraid that she would not believe me. I decided not to let my mother know what had happened, not ever.

My mother agreed to sit with me through the next class, but the day before the lesson I told her she did not have to come anymore, that I wanted to go by myself.

To this day I'm not sure why I did that. Maybe I was afraid that she would find out about the secret the devil and I were keeping. But that was a big mistake, for the devil now perceived my weakness. He saw that I did not have the courage or ability to resist.

From then on, he was even more depraved. As long as my mother didn't sit in, he was sure to use his "special method," over and over again.

One day, his fingers got closer and closer to my groin. I didn't know what to do, so I just kept on playing.

Finally, he thrust his fingers into my pants.

My body responded swiftly and violently out of a mixture of shame and fear.

"Look, it understands music!" the devil said in an inspirational voice. "Music has made it strong, peerlessly strong."

I did not dare to look down. Staring stubbornly ahead at the sheet music, I did not stop playing. But I did not know what I was playing. My cousin's wet body, with its shifting postures, appeared before my eyes. I seemed to be back with my face pressed against the frosted glass of the bathroom door.

I suspected that the devil already knew my secret. I had nowhere to hide.

My body was again on the verge of collapse. I pressed my legs close together, trying to prevent it, but it was already too late. That hot wave that had left me so red-faced once again spurted out of my body.

A smirk I'd never seen before appeared on the devil's face. Before I knew what was happening, the devil did something that left me feeling even more ashamed. He lowered his head and kissed the wet patch that had appeared on the crotch of my pants.

Impulsively, I stood up, grabbed my music, and rushed out of hell.

When I arrived home, I told my parents I wanted to study with my original teacher.

My parents asked me why.

I said I preferred to study with a lady.

"What difference does it make? At your age!" my mother said.

My father reprimanded me for not knowing what was good for me, and for disappointing my mentor, who had such high hopes for me.

They did not agree to let me switch teachers. They said that the big competition was approaching, the greatest challenge I had ever faced in my life. No matter what the reason, I should not change teachers at a time like this. My mother urged me to stick it out. My father said that sticking it out was the only way to defend my dignity as a piano prodigy.

That evening, the overwhelming sense of shame I felt left me completely unable to sleep. Strange visions ricocheted around in my head. I imagined that my little birdie had become a crawling caterpillar that got bigger and longer until it had become a boa constrictor. The boa constrictor wrapped itself around my feeble body. Every time I went somewhere I would see people pointing at me and gesturing. In a corner of the city square, a devil was holding up a torch, closing in on me. The boa constrictor

released me abruptly and started to grapple with the devil. After several rounds, a white flame flicked out of the
mouth of the snake, turning the devil into air. My strange
fantasy left my mind and body even more exhausted.

I even thought about killing myself, for the first time
in my life. I thought that only death could wash away
the intolerable shame that I felt. It was my cousin who
brought me back from the edge. In my worst desperation,
I suddenly thought of her. I thought of going to find her,
of telling her what I could not tell anyone. Before dawn,
I reached under my bed to retrieve the envelope with my
yearly allowance, which Chinese children receive every
Chinese New Year. Then I quietly snuck out the front
door.

At the entrance of our community was a taxi. I got in
and told the exhausted driver to take me to the train station. There I bought a ticket to Shilong.

As soon as I got on the train, I felt sleep instantly over-
take me, and I passed out, with my head resting against
the window.

By the time I woke up, or was woken up by the conductor, the train had already reached its destination in
Guangzhou. The lady conductor immediately discovered
that I had run away from home, and took me to the on-
board policeman, who turned me over to the railway police in the station.

My mother got the call, and rushed over right away to
take me home.

On the highway bus home, my mother peppered me

with questions, but I did not reply to any of them. I just rested my head against the window, my right hand mechanically playing the first few bars of the *Goldberg Variations* on the window, over and over. Then suddenly, a strange thought occurred to me. I decided to practice relentlessly and win a prize in the upcoming national piano competition. I knew that if I did our city would hold an award ceremony for me; I would stand on the podium with the devil. This was my chance. I would point at his bald head and tell everybody, "It's him!" The thought galvanized me. I told my mother that I no longer planned to switch teachers, but that I hoped she would still sit with me through every lesson. "We're covering too much ground now," I said. "I can't remember it all on my own."

Later on many things happened that everybody knows about. The opportunity I had created for myself arrived after I won the prize, but I did not have the courage to publicize my humiliation. My parents did not understand, and so all I could do was avoid it by going AWOL. As I hid in the power room, doubly ashamed now because of my withdrawal, I decided never to touch a piano again. I had to get away and stay away. I had to forget I had ever dreamed of becoming a pianist.

My decision did not surprise my parents. They did not colour or blanch. The last time I'd left home was still fresh in their memories, and they had a lingering fear I might do it again. After they found me back in my room, they went back to their own bedroom and had a heated argument.

My mother came out alone, walked over, rested her

hand on my shoulder, and reminded me tenderly that I should not waste time, that I should use every moment to review my schoolwork. She reminded me that the midterms were coming. From her exhortation, which had nothing to do with my decision to abandon piano, I knew the result of their argument: they would compromise. And that was the first time they had ever compromised with me.

Thirteen years have passed, and it's as if this all happened yesterday.

It was the death of the devil that reminded me of all of this.

I never again touched the piano after the night of the ceremony. I also gave up reading and chess and all my other hobbies. I became a kid that lacked interest in everything. My grades suffered, plummeted actually. Although I managed to do well enough to make it into the best high school in the city, once there my performance kept sliding. In the end I only managed to qualify for an average university located in the town of Shantou, majoring in secretarial work. In the first term of my third year, I became disgusted with my studies, and for a time felt like dropping out. But my parents' marriage was on the rocks, and I did not dare to make trouble for them. I knew that on the day when they had compromised with me regarding my decision, they'd opened up a rift between them, a rift which presaged the ultimate rupture in their relationship.

I managed to finish my studies. And after graduation

my father got me a job in a little agency in the municipal government. I worked there for over four years before transferring to a well-known real estate company where one of my mother's classmates from university worked as office manager. I have worked for her ever since.

Thirteen years. A pretty ordinary, uneventful thirteen years. In the end my parents got a divorce. Since then, no major events have occurred in my life. Of course sometimes people recognize me. And I've heard people discussing me behind my back or to my face. The most frequently heard expression is "What a pity." But it doesn't bother me at all when they judge me or when they sigh. They don't know the hellish darkness that I endured. They do not know the distress or desperation or despair I suffered on account of the angel, and then the devil. Nor do they know that I don't find it a pity at all. I don't care in the least that I was once a prodigy that everybody in the city knew. I don't care that now I am nobody.

Perhaps the psychological, or should I say physiological, change brought on by my "initiation"—which I found unfathomable at the time—was a major event in my life. In the past few years, people have often tried to set me up. But I've discovered that I no longer am interested in the opposite sex, I even feel a deep distaste. To me, girls are filthy and boring. I feel like they will sully me and disturb my daily routine. I even vaguely sense that this kind of psychological, or perhaps physiological, reaction is a kind of trauma or scar, the result of those two painful experiences thirteen years ago. But whether the angel or the devil was to blame, I'm not too sure.

Now the devil is dead. His death surely counts as a major event in my life. He took an overdose of antidepressants and died on the sofa where I had often sat: the site of many painful memories. I knew that after I stopped playing the piano, a major change occurred in the devil's life. He stopped accepting students. And he stopped serving as a judge. He stopped going out, or even taking calls. My mother would go to visit him twice a year, and she said his home was a smelly mess. She said many people had tried to help him find a woman to take care of him, but he refused all offers. She said in the past few years, he'd smoked and drunk a lot. He was suffering from a serious depression.

It was my mother who told me about the devil's death. She didn't expect that I would want to attend his funeral. She looked at me uncomprehendingly. In the past thirteen years I had never expressed any interest in the devil's situation. "Don't you know what kind of impact your decision to stop studying piano had on him?" my mother asked. "All this time I've felt guilty. He had such high hopes for you."

It would've been easy for me to turn my mother's guilt into hate. But I didn't feel like doing so. I did not feel like letting her know what the devil had done to me thirteen years ago, polluting and traumatizing me. The pollution was easily washed away when I got home, but the emotional scars I bear can never heal.

I've lived with these scars ever since. A very plain thirteen years it has been, and after all this time, I no longer hate him, not even a little. I'm even a little bit grateful to him. This was why I wanted to attend his funeral.

How could I be grateful? Had it not been for his fat fingers sending music into my pants—his own uniquely heuristic approach to pedagogy, as he described it—I would still be a prodigy today. I would still think of myself as a prodigy. And I would certainly still be dreaming the dream of a wunderkind.

But that was a dream my parents made me dream. It was a dream that our manic society made me dream. Truly, I'm now somewhat grateful to my mentor. His devilish conduct changed a prodigy everybody knew into a mediocre man. And that's all I am now. A mediocrity.

THE MOTHER

I decided not to see him off. He had not responded to my decision in any particular way. I just said I was tired. He seemed to want to say something, but in the end did not. He just got his bag ready.

The bag had been a birthday present from me, five years before. He had been using it ever since he tore off the wrapping paper, but he never said whether he liked it or not. He never said much about anything. He never said whether he liked anything I bought for him. Just as he had never said whether he liked me or not. He stuck a stack of crumpled documents into the bag. Then he patted his pockets to make sure he had not forgotten his wallet or his ID. This was his characteristic gesture of departure.

"Don't slack off on your homework!" he yelled in the direction of our son's room.

Our son had just asked me quietly whether he could come with us to the border inspection station. When I told him I wasn't going, he looked surprised. Then I reminded him that he had not finished his mathematics homework.

He found my reminder frustrating. He went back to his room, head down. The day before, his tutor had told me that despite a lot of practice, he had still not mastered the steps for converting repeating decimals into fractions.

My husband always slammed the antitheft door. For many years, I hadn't minded. That clanking sound, just like his taciturn character, had never bothered me. But the previous week when he left, I seemed to hear it for the first time, the intense impact. A sound to which I'd grown accustomed over many years suddenly became difficult, or impossible, for me to bear. On the way to the border, I did not say a thing. I did not even say, "Have a safe trip!" or "Watch your wallet!"—which was always the last thing I said before he went on his way. But the slam of the door last week still echoed in my ears, and my sudden distaste for it suppressed all other emotions. I did not want to say anything. I did not say anything.

At the gate, as usual, he said, "You go on home."

Which relieved me. I turned and walked away. Without saying a thing. I remember in the past whenever we parted, I would always walk away with a backward glance. He wasn't tall, and would be quickly submerged in the buzzing crowd. But I would look back anyway, believing I would somehow be able to see him, that he would be able to see me looking back at him.

I remember very clearly the way it used to be. But the

past couple of times, I had not been looking back at him anymore. I didn't remember when I stopped. It seemed very natural, very ordinary. And at first I didn't even notice. The last couple of times when we parted, I just walked away. In the crowded hall, I would occasionally look around at people coming my way, like curious foreigners or idle merchants. But I hadn't been looking back to see him off with my eyes. I'd been uneasy, in a hurry to get home to supervise our son, not wanting him to sit too long in front of the TV, hoping he'd work hard on his homework.

He did not react to the change in any particular way. This time, we parted outside the elevator. Like the week before, I did not say what I had always said in the past. He had lost his wallet once at the border crossing, and so I always used to remind him to watch his wallet. It had taken him nearly half a year to come to terms with that loss. He took it hard, not because he had lost the ID and bank cards it held, but because the wallet contained a picture of our son taken when he turned three. It was his favourite photograph. He worried that the person who had gotten his hands on the wallet would treat the photograph roughly, laugh coldly at it, or tear it up and toss it away. In his view, that would be a form of abuse of our son. It took him all that time to free himself from this fantasy.

Any time he mentioned our son, he would talk about what he was like when he was little, or how good he used to be. Usually not to praise our son's past, but to express dissatisfaction with the present. I didn't know whether this stubborn nostalgia of his meant that he didn't care about the child's development or that he cared too much. They hadn't really talked, had a real exchange, since the boy hit puberty.

I wondered why our son suddenly proposed that we see him off together. He was already twelve years old, and he had never made such a suggestion before. In all these years, the child would usually only see him on weekends.

His father was more a regular guest in his life than the father that fate had arranged for him. When they saw each other, he would ask our son whether he had had tests recently, and if so how he had done. But he apparently never looked forward to our son's answer. His questions were like small talk at a public gathering. Our son did not fear his father or hold him in awe, because his father didn't take responsibility for him or require anything of him. Relatives and friends all said that he was a good father— they also said he was a good husband—because he would always come back across the border every Friday night and take us to a fancy restaurant. Our son would always sit next to me. Sometimes I would take this opportunity to complain about him. He had not studied hard enough over the previous week or had watched too much TV. His father's reaction was always the same. He would stare at our son, then criticize him absentmindedly. "How could you?" or "That's unacceptable!" It was like he was staring at a subordinate and not his own son.

Often our son wouldn't say anything. But at times he complained, for instance about restaurant food not tasting as good as a home-cooked meal. He never wanted to go out to a restaurant, I knew. He didn't want to miss a certain television program he was obsessed with.

The clank of the metal door slamming had oppressed me all week long. It exacerbated my weariness with life. On the way back from the elevator, I walked right to the window in the family room and looked downwards in a daze. The square enclosed by the building complex was always occupied by pedestrians coming and going, by cars exiting or entering. I watched him walk quickly towards a waiting taxi.

For many years he, too, had been coming and going, in a monotonous, cold rhythm. I had no feeling at all anymore. But just now, I had suddenly decided not to send him off. I just said I was a bit tired. Actually I wasn't tired. I simply didn't feel like sitting with him in the taxi. Or more accurately, I didn't feel like sitting with him in silence, without even wanting to say a thing. So I decided not to send him off. I felt a bit lost and empty. In a way, I had moved the border closer to home; I had parted with him at the elevator. He had as usual slammed the door. And I had felt an extreme antipathy for the vicious metal clank, which sent my disgust with life to a new high. I never thought I would be so weary of life.

Our son's yell startled me. He shouted that his father had gotten into a taxi. I never thought that our son would be looking down from his room right then. A palpitation of self-remonstration rose through my brain, as I wondered why he had suddenly wanted to see his father off.

Maybe I should have let him. Maybe I should have gone with him.

I reminded him to use the time wisely and do his math homework. But I did not go to see whether he had returned to his desk. I did not want to leave the window, but longed to watch the taxi leave the curb and soon my sight. And I felt again the disturbance of anticipation in my body. Only this disturbance could allow me to step out of the shadow of my repression. As in the past, I covered my face in the curtain, as if afraid *he* would see me. As if last Thursday had not happened. Maybe he had never even seen me, I thought, embarrassed. Maybe he would never see me. I could still smell the dust on the curtain I'd never taken down and washed, for fear the smell would remind me of my own dusty youth, and of him, too. Every time I saw him walk my way, my youth would reappear; this hopeless awkwardness expanded in my weary bosom, stifling me.

The first time I'd seen him was at the celebration for the Mid-Autumn Festival held by our community. He was squatting, trying to guess the last lantern riddle, the one nobody solved, with his daughter. His hand was resting tenderly on her shoulder, his face practically stuck to hers. He was smiling, while she was deep in thought. I'd never seen such a radiant smile before, a smile that highlighted such a charming pair of lips. I seemed to have rediscovered anticipation, that feeling I had lost many years before. And the youthful awkwardness that had departed from my life also suddenly returned. It grabbed me viciously and wouldn't let go. I felt enfeebled. I did not know how I got through the crowd, through the lamp-light, through the noise, until finally I came back to the darkness of my quiet bedroom. I lay down on the bed, crossing my arms in front of my chest and dazedly rubbing my breasts, engorged still. I felt warm tears flooding my ear canal. I felt like time was ravishing me.

That was my first Mid-Autumn Festival, or so I believed. That was the first time in my life I'd ever seen anything so consummate, and from that day on I wanted to see him. It was the most overpowering thought I had ever experienced. I wished every day could be Mid-Autumn Festival. Every day at dusk I would walk close to the window, hide behind the faintly dusty curtain, and look down. Even on days when my husband returned home I would not want to miss the chance to indulge my gaze, heart pounding as I made out his form among the coming and going of the pedestrians. His arm was always around his daughter's shoulders. They were always talking. They always seemed to have so many things to say. I wished I could hear their conversation, like a passer-by who might join the discussion. I even imagined that there would come a day when they would start talking about me, allowing me into their world.

One day I finally got up the courage. I decided to walk over to them. I did not know the route they took for their daily stroll. But just as I walked out of the apartment tower, a mysterious wave of heat greeted me and allowed me to ascertain their position. I saw them immediately. I did not dare to walk right up to them. I just followed behind.

Looking at him from behind naturally elicited a despairing awkwardness that expanded in my chest, stifling me. I had to stop a few times to adjust my breathing, and in the end I simply couldn't stand it anymore. I had to stop completely. Regretfully, I watched them leave.

I took a deep breath of hot, humid air, turned, and started walking away, comforting myself in the most tender voice. I told myself I'd only wanted to approach, but the brief consolation soon became unbearable; I did not want to lie to myself like this. I knew I was getting farther and farther away from them, that I did not have the courage to turn and follow them again. I kept walking away. But my steps were getting slower and slower. I seemed to be walking into the depths of an ocean, an ocean of noise. It was getting harder and harder to breathe. Soon I could barely feel the stifling awkwardness. All I could feel was a tremble of despair. I despaired of us ever meeting in this city in reality. But at the same time I was sure that we would meet in some invisible city. There, I would walk over to him, and he would do the same. There, he would notice me notice him. I would amaze him with the temptation of my sheer existence. And there and then I would share a second spring with him.

Disheartened, I returned to my flat, by which time it was already the next day. Our son was fast asleep. I seemed to have returned from a space voyage, feeling like I was still floating, exhausted. I did not take a shower, just lay down. My body was pervaded with the same interplanetary scent that must waft through the galaxy. I wanted to keep this smell always. With my body, with my memory. Maybe not for him, perhaps, but for me. Through that smell I could sense myself. I did not know whether my husband had called—that was the first time (but not the last) that I didn't care whether he had called or not. But at the same time, I stood there expecting the phone to ring, out of sheer naivety. It was an unbearable expectation. I was waiting for it to ring, to dispel the despair and regret lurking deep in the night. That call would come from *him*, of course, and from another planet. I fantasized that he had already noticed me notice him, and that he would be able to decipher my gaze, discovering the secret path to my heart. I fantasized that he would reach towards my corner of awkwardness from another planet. And I fantasized that I would hear his breath and my own as well, and our breaths would meet in a perfect fusion, like water and milk.

I finally got to sleep, who knows when. When I was woken up by the phone, the hot sunlight was gathering on the hollow in the pillow beside me. I did not immediately think of my experience the night before, of my glide through space. I did not immediately think of the call I'd been expecting on a night of regret and despair. I picked up the phone like nothing was out of the ordinary. But the few strands of hair by the pillow made me uneasy.

The caller was a classmate of mine from middle school. Perhaps I should say he was my first love? But our special relationship was discovered soon after it started, by his mother. She was violently opposed. So after doing many things that humiliated me and my parents, she transferred her docile son to another school. We hadn't seen each other since. Even so, I recognized his voice immediately.

I was not at all curious about that voice. Nor did I feel an impulse to immediately hang up the phone. But I could hear he was emotionally distraught. "It's been almost twenty years," he said.

"I had not noticed," I said listlessly.

"You don't feel like that long has passed," he said.

"I hadn't bothered to feel anything," I said, unperturbed.

He said, "I feel like it's been even longer than that."

I picked up the few strands of hair by my pillow, and rubbed them between my thumb and my forefinger.

"I feel like it's been even longer than that," he repeated.

Then I suddenly smelled another planet. A feeling of the previous evening when I was gliding through space, anticipating the ring of the phone, resurfaced abruptly.

"That was such a good feeling," he said, all worked up.

"What feeling?" I asked.

"Don't you remember?" he asked.

"Yes," I said. "I remember I didn't feel anything at all."

My response did not cancel out the caller's interest in talking. He started going on about his life. He said he was unhappy. He said for many years he had only felt happy when he thought of me. I interrupted him several times and said I was not interested in hearing about his life, or anyone else's. But every time he segued back into his story. He said his wife was pretty good to him, but he still did not feel fulfilled. He also said his children were outstanding. But no matter what, his life wasn't what he'd hoped for. In the end I lost my patience and told him I was expecting my husband's call, hoping to cut him off for once and for all.

That did it. He had been interrupted. But he still did not hang up the phone. After a moment of silence, he entered upon a new round of conversation. He said that he had been pursuing me all these years. He asked me if I wanted to know how much of an ordeal it had been and how he had finally found my number. His voice was full of longing for my reply.

"I don't want to know anything," I said coldly and then hung up.

All I wanted to know was the situation on the other planet. I only wanted to see *him*. I just wanted to be able to pass by for one day. If noticing him was not enough to attract him, I would let out a long sigh to get his attention. Maybe I would need to sigh a number of times. Maybe I would need to pass by him a number of times. Maybe I would need to pass by and sigh many times before he would stop. I imagined him moving his hand away from his daughter's shoulder, stopping and asking me, curious, why I kept sighing like that. How would I reply? Would I say I was unhappy? Everyone said I had a happy life. I had a good husband. He was working on the other side of the border, working hard to support us. He came back every weekend and always took us to a good restaurant. Whenever I complained about our son, he always took my side. Maybe you could not say this was happiness. Maybe I really was unhappy. But I would not reply by saying that I was unhappy. I did not want to spoil the perfect feeling he gave me with the imperfection of my life. I might reply, "Because of you." Would this be a candid response, or would it be coy? I did not know. But I knew that as soon as I spoke, awkwardness would flood into my body again, until I was drenched in it. Maybe I really would get up the courage to say that the reason I sighed such long sighs was "because of you."

I never approached him. I never had the courage. I dared only to approach him by observation and expectation. Sometimes I would imagine a woman by his side, or wonder whether there was one. His daughter was my son's classmate. He had mentioned her several times. He said that her father was a professor of economics at the university. Her grandfather was a famous general. These details showed me how distant his world was from mine. I was not surprised that that smell of outer space had appeared that night. And I did not dread that smell. I did not mind it. I could not resist it. I longed for him to stop one day in front of me. I longed for him to stop to convey to me a mystery from another dimension.

The reason I suddenly decided not to send my husband off was because I was afraid I would miss the mystery. He had not appeared for four days straight. I was still looking forward to seeing him, looking forward to my shy awkwardness, looking forward to his return.

The last time I'd seen that girl was on a Thursday afternoon. On my way home from the market, I noticed a moving van stopped in front of their building. The girl was standing beside the van. I did not dare to stop and ask the onlookers what had happened. I just rushed home. I hid behind the curtain, fearful, assessing a situation for which I was not prepared. Soon I saw a small sedan drive up and stop beside the girl. Then the person inside opened the door, and she got in. I pressed the curtain against my quivering nostrils. I could not bear that sudden abuse. My vision grew blurry. Drowning in my tears, I could sense the car drive off. Then the truck began to move.

I kept standing there the whole time as though I were standing at the end of my life. I did not dare imagine how cold the coming nights would be. I did not dare imagine the next day.

I kept standing there until our son opened the door and came in. He hurried to my side and said, out of breath, "Something happened to someone in my classmate's family." He seemed to know that I knew perfectly well which classmate he was talking about.

"What happened?" I asked in despair.

He said he did not know. He looked at me in a daze, as if apologizing for my eyes, which were all red and puffy. "The teacher just said something happened," he said. "She has to move away immediately."

"She's already moved," I said to my son, blankly. To me, it was he who had already moved. I would never see him again from that window that had given me so much expectation, that had witnessed so much of my deep-seated awkwardness. The only place I could go to look for him now was in that imaginary city, where I would search aimlessly.

I believed that there would come a day when my conflicted sigh would hook his sense of smell like bait. He would stop. He would rest his hands lightly on my shoulders. His fingertips would hint, clearly yet unbelievably, that he would take me to a cozy room, onto a purple bedsheet. With his words and caresses, he would make me feel shy. Then he would penetrate my awkward shyness with his potent power, satisfying me, entrancing me, exhausting me.

I clutched at the curtain. I could still feel the warmth from the tears that were left on them Thursday at dusk.

My son came out of his room. "I saw him get in the taxi," he said, his tone lifeless.

"I saw too," I said with a smile, before pressing my cheek to the window again.

My son squeezed beside me, stood on his tiptoes, and looked down. "Do you always watch him from here?" he asked seriously.

His question made me very nervous. "Watch who?" I asked him uncomfortably.

My son seemed not to hear my question. "Why didn't you let me say goodbye?" he asked.

"Because you have to do your homework," I answered. I still wanted to know who the "him" in his question was.

"Then why didn't you say goodbye?" he asked.

I suspected my child knew my secret. A wave of sheer guilt swept towards me. I leaned down and held him close.

He pressed his warm cheek against my face, then backed away. He looked at me seriously and asked me whether I loved his father or not.

144

I did not know what to say. "Of course," I answered.
My son stuck his face to my face.

"Do you?" I asked.

"I don't know," he said. "Sometimes I love him, but sometimes I just don't know."

It was almost midnight before he called. Usually he called much earlier, when he got to his home in Hong Kong or soon after. This had been his habit over many years. "You forgot to remind me," he said over the telephone, as if chiding me, or maybe kidding.

"Remind you of what?" I was a little bit anxious. It surprised me that he would care about me.

He did not answer my question. He seemed to know the secret in my heart. "You forgot," he said. "The past two times you have forgotten."

I did not know how I should explain myself. I never thought he would notice the recent change in me.

"My wallet went missing again," he said. Now I could hear that he was chiding me.

"What happened?" I asked nervously.

"How should I know what happened?" he said calmly. "How should I know?"

For the past three days I had been imagining what happened in *his* family. I'd been wondering why he didn't appear on the day he moved. I'd been wondering who took that girl away, where she went. I'd been wondering why he would suddenly disappear from my sight, from my shyness, from my life. I had no idea what had happened in his life or in his family to make him so suddenly, so rudely disappear.

THE FATHER

Father calmed down gradually on the way back from the cemetery. Had he not insisted on staying until the end, we would not have witnessed an emotional collapse. Father had remained calm throughout this trying time, which to most people seemed hard to understand. In the crematorium, when he had said goodbye to mother's remains for the last time, my uncle whispered that he had not seen my father cry a single tear since my mother's death. "I'm really impressed by his self-control," my uncle said ironically, shooting my father a harsh glance. But when we placed her urn in the grave, Father was finally unable to contain himself. He suddenly started wailing. Everyone stared at him, including my uncle. He first looked at him and then at me, with a sly smile at the corner of his mouth, as if Father's sudden loss of emotional control was a response to his complaint to me in the crematorium.

I did not have time to protest. I embraced Father and urged him to restrain himself. Father did not pay any attention to my attempt to comfort him. He cried and cried, brushing my hands away. Distraught, he said that he should have been the one to put the first layer of dirt on the urn. I held my father's arm as he crouched beside the grave. I helped him cup a handful of dirt and sprinkle it on the urn with trembling hands. Then, on my relatives' advice, I helped him out of the grave and delivered him to the car so he could rest. When I had put father in the back seat, I advised him again not to cry. I said that his emotional outburst would have a big impact on all of us.

Father didn't say anything on the way home from the cemetery. He rested his head on the window, as if looking out at a mirage of the past. I adjusted the rearview mirror so I could keep an eye on him and saw him sitting quietly. His loss of control had taken everybody by surprise. But I believed that it was a good thing for him. Yes, ever since Mother's passing, nobody had seen Father shed a single tear. I really did not want him to bottle his sorrow up inside.

Before I had parked the car, Father said he did not need me to accompany him upstairs. He knew that I had a lot of follow-up to do. "You go and do what you need to do," he said calmly. But after getting out of the car, he gestured to me. He obviously had more to say. He walked around to my window. He held my left hand tightly with his hands. Another emotional impulse, perhaps. He said he hoped that my big brother and I could come home in the next couple of days. "I have some important things to tell you," he said.

I explained that when Mother was hospitalized, things

between my brother and me got really tense. I thought he should have noticed. My big brother had always been easygoing, and didn't like to have to deal with family matters. But when he learned that Mother had an incurable illness, his personality changed completely. He became fussy. He had an opinion on every detail in the planning of the funeral and disagreed with me on everything. I didn't think he would want to go home with me, or that he'd be interested in hearing what Father wanted to get off his chest.

My father shook his head helplessly. "To think that we used to be a model family," he said. "How could we end up this way?" It sounded like he blamed the family crisis on Mother's departure.

The next day at three o'clock I rushed to my father's place. I wasn't in a hurry to hear what my father wanted to tell me, I just didn't want him to worry himself unnecessarily if I were late. As I had reckoned, Father was up after his midday nap. His state of mind seemed a lot steadier than the day before. But before I sat down, he had already started to blame himself. He said that his outburst at the end of the funeral was unacceptable. He said he felt he had ruined the entire ceremony.

I did not agree with him. I said I felt just the opposite. I felt that, in expressing his true emotion, he had brought the entire process to its proper climax.

Father disagreed. He said my eulogy was the high point. Three people had been asked to speak. The first was the leader of my mother's work unit, a young man with a gut. He had actually never been my mother's colleague, because my mother had retired fifteen years before. And his eulogy, delivered in officialese, went on and on for thirty minutes. Father thought it was the most vapid eulogy. When the young man mentioned that Mother had served in the same work unit her whole working life, that she was a model of dedication, he used concrete figures to illustrate. He said that in her thirty-two years of work, Mother had never taken a day off, except for maternity leave. She only took three days off of sick leave, and every time she got sick she only took half a day off. Even the two postpartum leaves of absence she took were five days shorter than normal. These facts made the audience at the funeral click their tongues in amazement.

My father thought little of my uncle's eulogy. It was emotionally charged, but to him it sounded like a middle school student's composition. There were too many adjectives and too few facts. What my father was least impressed with was that, in addition to praising my mother as a good big sister, he also said she was a good wife and mother. My father did not think the little brother should be the one to declare that she was a good wife. And the only ones that should be able to say that she was a good mother were her own children.

My father thought that my own eulogy was a lot better than the first two. He said it was full of fine feelings and ample facts. In my eulogy I had discussed the last conversation I had with my mother before she passed away. My mother, strong-minded as always, said that she was satisfied with her life, mainly because she had a decent husband and two filial sons. She made a point of urging me to take good care of my father. She described herself as a workaholic, not as a good mother. She said that the honour of model family which the city had conferred upon us many times was a credit to my father's sacrifices and contributions. This part of my eulogy moved my father, who hadn't thought that at the very end, my mother would still care so much for him.

My father had never been a talkative guy; taciturnity had always been his style. He did not like to speak much in his work unit or at home. When my brother and I were in elementary and junior high school, he was always the parent at the parent-teacher day who spoke the least. His sudden loquaciousness surprised me. What was more, he had never talked about other people behind their backs, but now he started doing just that. I was shocked.

When he had finished assessing my eulogy, he looked at me solemnly. "Do you really think your mother was so perfect?" he asked.

Only then did I realize that my father was not completely satisfied with my eulogy. "Of course, she had her faults," I said.

"For instance?" Father asked, his tone and expression serious.

"Well, she always had to do everything herself. Just like she said, she was not a good mother," I said. "But she's not with us anymore. What's the point of saying these things now?"

"But there are some things that you can only say when someone has departed," my father said earnestly.

Now I wasn't just surprised at what my father had said, I was alarmed. Was he going to getting "important things" off his chest when some things are better left unsaid?

As expected, Father changed tack. "I only hit you guys one time. Do you still remember?" he asked.

Of course I remembered. It happened during summer vacation when I was nine years old. It was a Thursday afternoon. My brother asked me nervously whether I would go swimming with him. He told me he was going to turn thirteen in a few days. He wanted to go into the water once before his birthday and see what swimming was like, because he really hated that classmate of his for saying that anyone who had not been swimming by thirteen would suffer stunted growth. He did not need me to go into the water with him, or rather he needed me not to go into the water, in case something happened to him. If there was any danger, I could call for help on shore.

I understood my brother's trepidation, because in our family swimming was taboo. My father had always strictly forbidden us from going swimming, or even from mentioning swimming. He said it was too dangerous. He claimed he himself had never even thought about going swimming. I agreed to go with my big brother, out of curiosity but also for his own safety. But I reminded him to think about how to deal with Father. Because if Father found out …

My brother guaranteed that he would not find out.

He rode his bicycle with me on the back, past the well-known psychiatric hospital. Soon we arrived at a fairly large pond. My brother walked down the stone steps, obviously extremely timid and nervous.

"If Father finds out" and "If anything happens to him" echoed a duet in my head. I saw my brother standing on the final step. He made me turn away, and when he permitted me to look at him again, he was already in the water. I saw he had left his shorts on the final step. I don't know how long he stayed in the pond. I was worried about him the whole time, worrying about those two possibilities.

On the way home, my brother seemed extremely frustrated. He said that swimming was too difficult and that he might never learn.

I remember all of this very clearly.

Of course, the next memory was even clearer. That day, Father came home early from work because he knew we had gone out in the afternoon. As soon as he got in the door, he took down the feather duster—a murder weapon that mother would use to discipline us—from the back of the door. Father had always been much more patient than Mother. He had never been abusive. Naturally, we were shocked by his threat of physical punishment.

Father ordered us to stand in front of him. He asked my brother where he had taken me on his bike that afternoon. On the way home, we had run into a colleague of my father's. It must have been he who ratted us out.

My brother gave the explanation he had prepared, saying we'd gone to a classmate's home near the psychiatric hospital.

Father turned to stare at me.

I was trembling head to toe, nervous that the first "what if" would come true. Instinctively, I nodded.

Father suddenly lost control. The duster smacked down on my arm. And then it smacked down on brother's back, over and over again. We had never seen Father get so angry before. As he hit my brother, he berated us for breaking the rule against swimming, and even worse for lying to him about it.

Protecting his head with his hands, my brother quoted from Chairman Mao's *Little Red Book*, saying that Father had not sought truth from facts, and that "he who makes no investigation and study has no right to speak."

Then Father said something we did not understand. After he said it he gave my brother another couple of hard lashes on the back.

"What did I say?" my father asked, curious. I did not expect that he had forgotten the strange, confusing, and scary words he had uttered. Father gave me a sincere look, obviously wanting to know what he exactly he had said in the heat of anger that day.

"You said that you smelled death on us," I told Father. "You said that this was seeking truth from facts."

My father laughed wryly, as if he was making fun of his own memory.

Then I told Father that my brother and I had often discussed it afterwards, but had never been able to figure out what he'd meant, or what that had to do with our secret swimming outing.

My father adjusted his sitting posture. "That's what I have to tell you about now," he said solemnly.

Father's tone of voice intimated the importance of what he had to say. I leaned forward a bit, as if to get closer to my father's memory. I anticipated that my father's narration would set off a chain reaction. It might change our relationship.

"I was not always a person who, as your mother put it, knew my place. I used to be lively and talkative. I only changed a few days after I got married," he said. "Your mother actually fell in love with me because I had a rebellious streak. Just like all the other girls that liked me."

"I knew that you were the college champion in the hundred-and-ten-metre hurdles. And that for a lot of female classmates you were a heartthrob," I said. Mother had mentioned lots of times that Father had been pursued by many girls at university.

"But I bet you don't know that I was also on the varsity swimming team," Father said. "Track and field came later on, because the director of athletics thought that I had more potential to make the school proud in track and field."

I was shocked. "Didn't you always tell us that you never even thought about learning to swim?" I asked.

Father did not reply to my question. "At seventeen, I attended a municipal swimming competition," he said. "I came fifth in the hundred-metre freestyle."

I could not accept the appearance of a different father from the one I had always known. It was as hard to accept as Mother's departure. I didn't know why my life had suddenly turned into a total farce. "What's going on?" I said, aggravated. "You told us that you never ever thought about learning to swim."

My father was obviously prepared for my question. "Everything changed at noon that day," he said calmly.

I saw the same look in his eyes as he had had on the way back from the cemetery. He seemed to be gazing at scenes from an inescapable past.

"It was the fifth day of our married life," he said. "We were on our honeymoon, which we spent in your mother's hometown. That day at noon, your mother took me to see that famous reservoir, and we went for a walk on the path around it. Your mother told me anecdotes from her childhood, one after another. She had an elementary school teacher who went on to marry a war hero. Her father was bitten by a poisonous snake one time when he was trying to catch mudfish, and to save himself, he scooped away a hunk of flesh from around the wound. And when the postman knew her father was not at home, he would stay and chat with her mother; he seemed always to have more to say to her."

"The beautiful scenery around the reservoir, and your mother's wonderful stories, made me feel that life in a country village would be simple and agreeable, and that life in the good old days was so much less complicated. An honest sense of belonging arose in my heart. It was an even better feeling than the one I'd had on my wedding night, when I held your mother tight as we went to sleep. I couldn't help myself—I held your mother's hand. You should know that in our day and age, for a man and a woman to hold hands in public was considered uncouth. It was in bad taste, something the petty bourgeois would do. But at that specific moment, I felt that holding her hand was very natural. And very innocent. I believed the feeling would be mutual."

Father and Mother had never expressed affection for one another in front of us. I could not imagine them walking hand in hand.

"That feeling gave me an intense desire for intimacy. To have such an urge in broad daylight gave me an anguished sense of guilt, like I was breaking the law. In that day and age, such a desire wasn't just low class, but also dirty. It was for hooligans. But I couldn't help myself. I turned and embraced your mother, and placed my lips upon hers," Father said. "Right then, we heard the sound of someone calling for help. It's a sound that I can still hear today. It was the sound of two children. It came from our right-hand side, from the shore, not far away from where we stood. The two children had a companion who was struggling for his life in the reservoir, about a hundred-and-fifty metres from shore. I would have needed just over a minute to swim to his side. I released your mother and prepared to dive in."

My father kept staring ahead, as if he had not left the scene. I anxiously waited for him to relate how he had saved the child.

"I did not expect that your mother would react as she did. She held me tight. She would not let me go. 'What happens if something happens to you?' she asked severely," Father said. "She must've known that nothing would happen to me. I was a very good swimmer and had adequate life-saving skills. There was no way anything could happen to me. But if I did not take action immediately, something was certain to happen to the child. I slipped out of your mother's grasp."

I was on edge. I wished he would hurry up and get to the end of it.

"But before I had managed to walk a step, your mother had knelt down on the ground and wrapped her arms around my legs," Father said. "'You're so irresponsible,' she said. 'We've only been married for five days and now you're going to abandon me.' And then she started hitting the ground with her head, as if she was in such agony that she did not want to live."

I couldn't connect my mother in my father's story to the mother I had known at all.

"The sound of the cries for help made me frantic. I begged your mother to let me go. I told her that it was my urgent duty to go and save that child. Surprisingly, your mother suddenly did as I had asked. She stood up, brushed the dirt off her pants, and said with icy calm, 'You go. I won't stop you. I won't stand in your way. If you think that that stranger in the reservoir is more important than your own wife, then go.' This was obviously not a change in her attitude, but a change in tactics. I couldn't stand it. I realized that if I took action, leapt in to save the boy, I might have to sacrifice our marriage. I started shaking all over. I felt weak and craven. I did not even have the courage and energy to move my feet. Your mother continued with her reverse psychology. 'Go on, then. I'm not stopping you or anything,' she said. 'It doesn't matter whether you care about me or not.' Her calmness, or should I say coldness, horrified me. Suddenly I felt totally blocked, emotionally," Father said. "When I had recovered, your mother was already a long way off, walking towards the bus stop. I glanced at the reservoir, then at the two children who were still calling for help. My heart was full of fear. Eventually, in despair, I ran to your mother."

This dramatic ending made my heart sink. I did not know how to comfort my father, still less how to comfort myself.

"Do you know how I made it through that night? That was the first sleepless night of my marriage, the first night on which I felt no sense of security. Your mother and I took the same public bus, but she refused to talk to me. She refused to talk to me even after we got home. She turned her back on me the entire evening," Father said. "I was shivering in the night, hearing the cries for help of those two children in counterpoint with the calculatingly indifferent tone in your mother's voice. We'd been married five days, and marriage had already caused me incredible shame. I already sensed that I would live with the shame for the rest of my life. In just five days, marriage had already filled me with dread."

My father's words made me feel that Mother's funeral had not ended. Father should have delivered a eulogy. And his eulogy would have been the grand finale.

"The next day at dawn, I returned alone to the reservoir. Only a dozen hours before, I had felt a powerful longing for intimacy there, but after my first sleepless night of marriage, your mother was now a stranger. Dazed, I looked at the quiet and cold surface of the reservoir. I had a sudden urge to wade in," Father said. "Before I was in up to my knees, a farmer carrying a load of manure walked by on the path. He shouted that it was very deep in the middle. 'People drown in the reservoir every year,' he said. 'Just yesterday a middle school student died there.'"

I couldn't help calculating that if Father had saved him, that child would already have reached the age of retirement.

"People say that everyone has an experience in their life that is the most important to them. And for me, this is it. From then on I became reticent. I became a person who knew his place. And from then on I shouldered almost all domestic duties," Father said. "Your mother never mentioned the episode again. Had she not predeceased me, you would never have known about it. And I don't know whether you should know about it. I don't know what, if anything, it has to do with you."

I thought about the last thing Father had said. It seemed to me that even though it had happened before we were born, before we were even conceived, it still had something to do with us. No doubt about it. It had not only complicated our conception and birth, but also affected us as we were growing up, shaping the taboos of our childhood. It was part of our lives, or our lives were a part of it.

"People may have different opinions about my loss of control at your mother's grave. But nobody could know that I was in fact crying for another person, who's been dead for nearly fifty years. I think he might be the first person your mother met in the underworld," Father said. "I think he has already forgiven her. I even think that they might become soul mates."

I was certain, however, that Father had not forgiven her. Otherwise, why would he tell me about a trauma that had brought shame upon his marriage? I don't know whether he'd ever had a moment during his married life when he thought that he might have died trying to rescue that boy. Might such a realization have made him grateful to my mother for holding him back? I did not want to ask him. Nor did I dare.

"Now you know why you had such a sheltered upbringing, why I always kept such a close eye on you," Father said. "In getting married, your mother and I had tied the knot with death. I have spent every moment of our marriage worrying about karmic retribution, and I think that this is reflected in your mother predeceasing me. I believe it is fate for you and your brother to know about what happened. Maybe, in time, other people will learn."

I handed my father two napkins. He glanced at me, but showed no sign of wiping the tears from his eyes.

"Actually there are many possibilities, and we can make various hypotheses about the incident. The hypothesis I've spent the most time considering is that if I had gone to save that child and nothing had happened to me, your mother might not have followed through on her threat to divorce me. She might have soon forgiven me for abandoning her, or for doing my duty by the boy. Our marriage might have survived, and you might have still come into the world. Another possibility is that your mother would have remained aloof, as on the night of the incident. In this case, I have often wondered, would we have been able to carry on?" Father said.

"The second evening, her attitude toward me totally changed, completely unexpectedly. As soon as I lay down in bed, she grasped my hand, and begged me to hold her. My heart palpitated violently. I thought that my heart and mind would stop me from responding in kind, because such reciprocation would have indicated that I was already over the feeling of estrangement that the incident had brought on. It would be as if I'd crossed the line between life and death. I never thought I would do that so calmly. I turned on my side, and laid my hand on your mother's hip. She tapped my nose with her forefinger. 'I know you would never leave me,' she said warmly, her voice full of emotion."

I gestured for my father to wipe away the tears that were about to fall.

"But on the way back from the cemetery, I thought of another possibility," Father said. "Had I not dared, had I been reluctant to cross over that threshold, had I brutally brushed her loving hand away, what then? What would have become of us?"

I put my right hand on my father's knee. I wanted to tell him that Mother wasn't there with us anymore. You two are now forever separated by that brutal line. What's the point of mentioning all of this now?

THE TAXI DRIVER

The taxi driver drove into the company parking lot and saw his space was taken. He did not even glance at the licence plate, but saw another space on the north side and parked there. The taxi driver got out and looked around. He walked to the end of the car, opened the trunk, and took out a backpack with just a few odds and ends in it. He lightly closed the trunk, muttered something, and tapped the lid twice. Then he looked up. A raindrop fell on his face.

The taxi driver would normally have noted the number of any car parked in his spot. The next time he took the car out he would have chewed out whichever colleague had parked it there. "What the hell is wrong with you?" he would have yelled in a venomous voice. But just now he hadn't bothered to check. He walked into the office and gave the keys to the old man on duty. The old man gave the taxi driver an apprehensive glance and immediately looked away, as if afraid that the taxi driver would see the look on his face. The taxi driver hesitated a moment, then patted the old man on the shoulder. The old man got all choked up. "Those poor girls," he said in a trembling voice.

The taxi driver seemed not to hear. He calmly turned and would have just walked out, had the old man not cried out for him to stop. He looked back.

The old man poked his head through the office window and called, "The manager wants you to come on Thursday to do the paperwork."

"Got it," the taxi driver said in a low voice, as if talking to himself.

The rain still would not fall. The air was oppressive. The taxi driver walked along the crosstown street towards his home. It was still rush hour. Many cars had their brights on; an awful glare.

The taxi driver crossed two streets and reached the entrance to the biggest pizzeria in town, which is where the woman had hailed him when he was driving past at the end of his shift. There were only two patrons inside. In this bustling city, this restaurant was always nearly deserted, which was exactly the kind of atmosphere he wanted right now. He needed peace and quiet.

The taxi driver ordered a large cola and a seafood pizza, his daughter's favourite. As he ordered the pizza, his eyes filled with tears, blurring his vision. The cashier had to remind him three times before he realized he hadn't paid. He quickly got out the money and handed it over. "Sorry," he said, a bit choked up.

The taxi driver sat at a table by the window. His

daughter sometimes sat across from him. She was always in a hurry to take the first bite when the pizza arrived, and it'd be so hot that it burned her tongue, making her gasp for cool air. Then she would roll her tiny eyes and smile a silly smile. From that seat, the taxi driver could see a busy street scene, watching the cars file past in an endless stream. He had made his living in this environment for fifteen years. Every day he would shuttle down busy city streets in his taxi. He was familiar with that, inured to it. But a few days ago, he suddenly felt he wasn't so used to it anymore. The same thing with the lot. Where before he would check the licence plate of anyone who dared to park in his space, now he did not feel it belonged to him, or that he belonged in the lot. He no longer had to bother, because he would never take the taxi out again.

Before he drove the taxi into the parking lot, he had already had his last fare as a taxi driver. At dusk, he had been worried it was going to pour, worried because the windshield wipers weren't working, worried he would be forced to end his last day at work early, which he didn't want to do. Maybe he still felt attached to his occupation, or maybe he felt attached to the taxicab that had accompanied him all these years. The taxi driver's wish came true. It didn't end up raining. Just as he was bidding his taxi adieu, a drop of rain fell on his face.

The taxi driver wiped away the tears in his eyes and had a big gulp of his cola. Lost in thought, he seemed to once again see the woman with the grave expression as she had gotten into his taxi at the entrance to the pizzeria.

He had asked her where she wanted to go.

She said go straight.

The taxi driver was puzzled. He asked where exactly she wanted to go.

Again, she wanted him to go straight.

The taxi driver glanced at the woman in the rearview mirror. Her attire was formal, her expression solemn. She obviously had something on her mind.

Soon, her cell phone rang. The woman seemed to know that the phone would ring just at that time. She got it out of her purse in a leisurely way, apparently displeased with the interruption to her thoughts. "Yes, I know," she said.

The taxi driver gave her another glance in the rearview mirror.

"What else can I do!" the woman said.

The taxi driver could hear from her simple reply that she was distraught.

"Maybe that's it," the woman said.

The taxi driver saw she had turned her head and was looking out the window.

"I don't want it to be this way," the woman said.

A kind of mystified curiosity stirred in the taxi driver's soul. He started to imagine what kind of person would have made such an upsetting call to his customer.

"You couldn't imagine," the woman said.

No, the taxi driver could not imagine. It must be a man she was talking to. But then he felt that it was also very likely it was a woman. In the end he even thought it might be a child. This final thought made his steering wheel shudder.

"You're completely wrong," the woman said.

The taxi driver thought of his own daughter. In the past week, every time he'd answered the phone he had hoped to hear a miracle, a child's voice from another world. He did not know whether his daughter would still call. It was a call he imagined in his despair.

"No way," the woman said.

Perplexed, the taxi driver glanced at her in the rearview mirror. He noticed her sexy hair.

"You'll never get it, will you?" the woman said.

The taxi driver slowed down. He was worried that the woman might miss her destination.

"There's no reason to worry," the woman said.

The taxi driver found her resolute voice difficult to bear. He wanted to interrupt her and ask her where she was going.

"I will tell you," the woman said. She was clearly tired of talking. She said goodbye impatiently. Then she put her cell phone back into her purse. She looked at her watch, then at the clock in the cab. Her expression was still solemn. "Let me out after the next intersection," she said coldly.

The taxi driver felt relieved. He stepped on the gas and angrily passed the truck that had been blocking his way.

As soon as the taxi came to a stop, she passed him a hundred yuan note. Then she opened the door and got out. The taxi driver called to tell her to wait for her change. But the woman did not stop. Her seductive hair made the taxi driver feel a rare moment of loneliness.

The taxi driver had viewed that woman as his very last fare. That's what he had been thinking, looking her over in the rearview mirror. He was happy that his final passenger had stirred his imagination and hope with half a conversation. But right when he was calling out to his last customer to say he would make change, about half of what she'd handed him, another two passengers, a couple, got into his taxi. They were going to a place not far from the parking lot of the taxi company. The taxi driver hesitated but did not refuse them.

This couple were very concerned about the amount of space between them, as the taxi driver noticed from the start. He also noticed that the man was about to say something several times, but was stopped short each time by the cold look on the woman's face. Apparently she was the one who was keeping her distance. The rush-hour traffic was chaos. There were accidents on several major arteries. The worst one was on the northwest corner of the midtown square. They were stuck there for the longest time. When the driver at last managed to make it through, the man finally broke through the line of ice. "Sometimes I miss …," he said haltingly.

"Sometimes?" the woman said harshly. "What is there to miss?"

Her reply got a rise out of the man. "Right," he said ruefully. "Everything seems wrong."

"How can right possibly seem wrong?" The woman

said, her tone still severe.

The road was so heavily congested it was hard to make any headway at all. The taxi driver had even more free time to wonder about this couple, but he reminded himself not to keep looking in the rearview mirror. To keep his mind on something else, he forced himself to think about the woman passenger just before. He felt that her caller could not have been a child in fact, because the woman's expression was so serious from beginning to end, her tone so cold. At the thought, he felt frustrated. For the past week, he had been waiting for a child's voice, full of life, to call him from another world.

The man and woman were still engaged in a difficult dialogue. The man's voice was faint, the woman's harsh.

"I really don't understand why ..."

"You've never understood."

"Actually ..."

"Actually that's just the way it is. You'll never understand."

"Can't we find or try to think of some other way?"

"Can we? Is there any other way?"

Due to the weakness of the man's voice, the conversation never turned into an argument. But it never made any headway, either. The woman met all his questions with the same severity, keeping the conversation stalled at whatever starting point the man had managed to find.

"Don't assume ...," the man said finally, distraught. He was obviously trying to give the stuck conversation one last push.

"I did not assume," the woman replied, cutting him off again.

The taxi driver had put the car into neutral and stepped lightly on the brake. The taxi came to a stop at the location the man and woman had indicated. This woman also passed him a hundred yuan note. When the taxi driver looked back to give her change, he discovered her cheeks were covered in tears.

Sitting in the pizzeria, the taxi driver remembered how he used to pass a napkin to his daughter. "Wipe your face," he would say impatiently. Most of the time, she would sit across from him, her lips covered in sauce. The taxi driver had always been careless. He had never much cared about the expressions on his daughter's face, or about her existence. He was the same with his wife. He'd never imagined that they might cease to exist. But in an instant, they had. A void had suddenly appeared in his life, leading the taxi driver to a sudden discovery of the past they all shared.

For the past week, he had been grieving, diving deep into his memories. Just like that, his world had lost its most essential voice, becoming unbearably quiet. But he could not keep his thoughts quiet. His nights were sleepless, as long-neglected moments in his life suddenly became vivid, crashing into his heart. He didn't even have the courage to go to his own house, not anymore. He was afraid of a house that was no longer a home. He was afraid of a pitiless silence that would stifle his memories. In the past week, he had turned into a careful fellow, replaying the past in his imagination in every detail.

The taxi driver knew he was in a dangerous mental state. He quit his job. For the past week he'd seen his daughter and wife over and over, as they kept inviting him to revisit their shared past. The life he had never really cared about suddenly became full of colour and drama. He filled in their expressions and their gestures with a fine-grained memory. He did not want to miss a thing. Of course he wouldn't want them to just appear one day in front of the taxi. He would freeze at the sight of their terror-stricken faces, unable to react in time. He would slam on the brake, knowing it was already too late. He would be in unbearable pain. He was in unbearable pain. Wrongly assuming he was the person who had caused the accident, he sank into an abyss of self-reproach. Only when a truck appeared in his field of vision would the truth drag himself out of the abyss. Irate, he would step on the gas and pass the truck.

The taxi driver had been on the road from Shenzhen to Guangzhou, en route to the fare of a lifetime, when a truck carrying a load of books ran over his wife and daughter.

The taxi driver finished his pizza in the tangle of his thoughts. He recalled the way his daughter looked when he was eating and how his wife used to sit to the side, teasing them happily. The taxi driver finished the last sip of his cola, got the ice cubes out of the paper cup, and arranged them in a row on the table. This was a game his daughter had liked to play. He couldn't bear now to see that line of ice. He closed his eyes and saw his daughter's thin finger moving over the tabletop, a gesture that had seemed meaningless at the time but was so deeply meaningful to him now. The taxi driver opened his eyes and turned his head to look dazedly out the window at the busy streetscape. The familiar scene suddenly seemed uncanny, so much so that his heart ached. He'd spent the past fifteen years shuttling through those city streets day and night, and he hadn't left a single trace.

He was sure he could not go on living in such a foreign city. He decided to move back to the countryside, to take care of his aging parents and keep them company, and also because he believed that only their presence could quiet his mind. Fifteen years had passed since he had left them. His reappearance might seem like his resurrection—a miracle, it would seem to them. He looked forward to the satisfaction he would give them. He even fantasized that in fifteen years, a similar miracle would see his daughter and wife also return to his side. Yes, he would go back to his hometown, where, he hoped, he could reclaim the meaning of his life and find the peace and quiet he so desperately needed.

His last passenger had given the taxi driver's mood a bit of a boost. He was surprised to discover that he was still curious about life. His sense of hearing had been eroded by extreme sorrow, but his ears continued to function. He could still hear other people's voices. And he was still curious about them. Yes, he'd actually heard what the

old fellow at the company office had said so emotionally: "Those poor girls!" At the time the taxi driver had
shuddered, but he hadn't made any reply. He had quietly
turned and walked away, as if he had not heard the old
man's agonized sigh. He was afraid to hear it. He was
afraid of himself. He'd chosen to leave his life behind,
and had resolved to refuse the company's compassionate
request for him to stay. After signing the paperwork on
Thursday, he would no longer be a taxi driver. The decision had been made.

The taxi driver turned his head from the uncanny
street scene. Up ahead, not far away, were a mother and
daughter, who didn't seem to catch his eye. He stared at
the table in front of him. He discovered that the row of
ice cubes had already melted. Affectionately, he stroked
the melted water on the table with his fingertips, as if
stroking the ethereal past.

Suddenly his fingertips touched his daughter's. He
heard her piercing laugh. He heard his wife ask why she
was laughing so happily, but their daughter did not reply.
Her soft fingertips pressed against his, as if to invite him
to play their familiar game. He accepted, and pressed his
fingertips against hers, causing her fingers to withdraw
slowly in the ice water until they reached the edge of the
table. In the last instant the taxi driver felt that disaster
was upon him. He wanted to grasp his daughter's lively
little impish hand, but could not.

The taxi driver knew he had missed his chance and
would not get another. This was the last time he and his

daughter would ever get to spend time together in the city. He would never again touch the tabletop in the pizzeria. He would leave the city, never to return. To the city, which to him had become suddenly strange, it was as though he were already gone, as though he had departed with his wife and daughter; as though they had all disappeared together. Their going gave the taxi driver a serenity he had never felt before, a sense of peace and quiet that was of an incomparable purity. This sacred sensation, which had appeared earlier than he had expected, moved the taxi driver so much that he burst into tears.

ACKNOWLEDGEMENTS

Having published many books in Chinese, I am grateful to those who have allowed me to realize to my dream of publishing in English: publisher Linda Leith, whose passion for literature is embodied in every detail of the book; translator Darry Sterk, who has turned the original Chinese into elegant English with the skill of a magician; the extraordinary Chinese illustrator Cai Gao, who has a profound understanding of my characters; Radio-Canada international journalist Yan Liang, who introduced me to my publisher and my translator; and Carole Channer, a friend fascinated with literature and the English language, who read the manuscript and whose comments on it encouraged me.

And I owe special thanks to Ha Jin, winner of the National Book award, for the insights and support that have helped me create a bridge between my writing and my new audience.

RECYCLED
Paper made from
recycled material
FSC® C100212
www.fsc.org

Printed in July 2016
by Gauvin Press,
Gatineau, Québec